One Summer in Vancouver

One Summer in Vancouver

Tony Correia

James Lorimer & Company Ltd., Publishers
Toronto

James Lorimer & Company Ltd., Publishers acknowledges funding support from the Ontario Arts Council (OAC), an agency of the Government of Ontario. We acknowledge the support of the Canada Council for the Arts, which last year invested $153 million to bring the arts to Canadians throughout the country. This project has been made possible in part by the Government of Canada and with the support of Ontario Creates.

Cover design: Tyler Cleroux
Cover image: Shutterstock, iStock

Library and Archives Canada Cataloguing in Publication

Title: One summer in Vancouver / Tony Correia.
Names: Correia, Tony, author.
Identifiers: Canadiana 20220485062 | ISBN 9781459417168 (softcover) | ISBN 9781459417236 (hardcover) | ISBN 9781459417434 (epub)
Subjects: LCGFT: Novels.
Classification: LCC PS8605.O768 T43 2023 | DDC jC813/.6—dc23

Published by:
James Lorimer & Company
Ltd., Publishers
117 Peter Street, Suite 304
Toronto, ON, Canada
M5V 0M3
www.lorimer.ca

Distributed in Canada by:
Formac Lorimer Books
5502 Atlantic Street
Halifax, NS, Canada
B3H 1G4
www.formaclorimerbooks.ca

Distributed in the US by:
Lerner Publisher Services
241 1st Ave. N.
Minneapolis, MN, USA
55401
www.lernerbooks.com

Printed and bound in Canada.
Manufactured by Friesens Corporation in Altona, Manitoba, Canada in February 2023.
Job #294589

For Billeh Nickerson
Because he's a professional.

"The Games are really not about athletics. They're about a statement on the quality of our lives."

Dr. Tom Waddell,
Founder, Gay Games

West End Vancouver

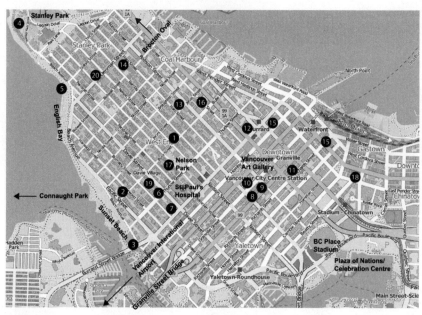

① The Green House on Bute Street	⑦ Celebrities Nightclub	⑬ Empire Landmark Hotel/ Cloud Nine	⑰ Raven's Apartment Building
② Dwayne's house	⑧ Orpheum Theatre	⑭ West End Community Centre	⑱ The Lotus
③ Vancouver Aquatic Centre	⑨ Commodore Ballroom	⑮ Simon Fraser University Downtown campus	⑲ Ming Court Hotel
④ Second Beach Pool	⑩ Fluevog	⑯ The Elbow Room	⑳ The Grove Inn
⑤ Bikini Beach	⑪ A&B Sound		
⑥ Little Sisters Book & Art Emporium	⑫ Burrard Skytrain Station		

Saturday, July 28, 1990

Bute Street

If anyone asks me, I'll blame it on the Village People. They're the reason I went to the airport instead of my part-time job. I'll blame them and the Greatest Hits cassette Mom left in my car. If it weren't for the Village People, I'd still be home in Mississauga, stocking shelves at Safeway. Instead, I'm standing on a street in a city I've only ever seen on *21 Jump Street*.

I wipe sweat from my eyes. Sunlight reflects off the ocean at the bottom of the hill, so bright I need my aviators to see. My jeans chafe against my sweaty thighs. I'd love to run into the water to cool off.

I'm standing in a forest of concrete apartment buildings. One balcony is playing Madonna's "Vogue." Another plays

"Love Will Never Do Without You" by Janet Jackson. The coconut scent of Hawaiian Tropic suntan lotion sticks to the air like humidity. It's Mom's favourite brand. Mom. She's got to be worried sick about me.

"Are you lost?"

It's hotter than hell and he's dressed all in black. Short-sleeved button-down shirt, black denim shorts, dress socks rolled into doughnuts above his Doc Martens, and a hat like Zorro. I think he's wearing lipstick and eyeliner. The only colour on him is the bright yellow Sony Walkman attached to his hip.

"Pardon?" I say.

"Pardon?" he says sarcastically. "What are you, a Boy Scout?"

"I used to be."

He examines me like I'm a piece of art. Like he's trying to figure out what I'm about. I feel naked and strange. He laughs and I don't feel so awkward.

"You look lost is all I'm saying. You need directions?"

"Do you know where this is?" I show him the page I ripped from the phone book at the airport. I point to my uncle's address for Zorro to see.

"That's the green house on Bute Street! My friend's friend lives there," he says. "Right street, wrong turn. I can take you there if you want. It's on my way to work."

"Do you mind?" I ask. "I have no idea where I'm going."

"Where are you from?" Zorro asks.

"Ontario. Mississauga."

"You're either straight or closeted because you didn't say Toronto. You here for the Gay Games?"

"Do I look gay to you?"

Zorro backs up, arms raised.

"Hey dude, I'm not accusing you of anything. The Games are literally a week from today. It's an honest question."

Crap. I freaked him out.

"Sorry," I tell him. "Yeah, I'm here for the Gay Games. But not to compete. I only found out about them a few days ago. There were pamphlets at The 519."

"That the Gay Community Centre in Toronto?"

"Yeah. I was kind of checking it out." I don't know why I'm covering my tracks. It's not like I'm ever going to see this guy again. "I came here sort of last minute."

"How last minute?" he asks.

"Like six hours ago. My parents don't know where I am. My uncle has no idea I'm here."

Zorro looks at me with equal parts wonder and concern. "Wow. Go big or go home, eh?" he says. "I'm Dwayne."

He holds out his hand for me to shake. I look at it like it's diseased.

"Tom," I say, shaking his hand with intention, like Dad taught me.

Dwayne guides me up the hill to my uncle's house. The street is tree-lined and pretty. I forget that I'm in another city. And that my parents still have no idea where I am.

Bute Street

Rusty hinges squeak as I push the gate open. The paint on the porch steps is worn off from all the footsteps. It's cooler under the awning. The screen door lets what breeze there is into the house. Joni Mitchell is playing softly from inside. I press the doorbell.

He's a shadow at first, backlit from the sun that's coming through the back door. It's not until he gets closer that my uncle comes into focus. Curly, straw-coloured hair and eyebrows. Freckles and blue eyes. A thinner version of Dad. He's wearing a pair of cutoff khaki shorts and a faded iron-on t-shirt that says, "No, *I'm* the Rhoda."

Uncle Fred leans against the doorframe without opening the screen door.

"Are you who I think you are?" he asks.

"It's me, Uncle Fred, your nephew Tom."

"The nephew who never writes or calls?"

"That's me," I say, like it's a joke. "Is it okay if I stayed here for a bit?"

"No," he says. I see him walk into a room off the hall.

He's joking right? He wouldn't leave me standing here on the porch. I remember the last time I saw him. I was ten and hid behind my mother when he bent down to say hello. I've only heard from him on birthdays and Christmas since then. He sends a card every year. Each one with a twenty-dollar bill inside. He owes me nothing.

"Come on in," Uncle Fred says, coming back into the hall. "Sorry. I didn't want you thinking I'm a pushover."

I follow my uncle down the hall to the kitchen. He opens the fridge and starts pulling out different kinds of cheeses, pickles, olives, and crackers. He pours me a glass of Perrier.

"Now, will you kindly explain what you are doing here?" Uncle Fred says, sitting next to me at the kitchen table.

An avalanche of footsteps comes thundering down the stairs. A guy who doesn't look much older than me enters the kitchen, both arms straddling the doorway like he's keeping us there. He's tanned, lean, and muscular, like a model in the Calvin Klein underwear ads. The sleeves of his plaid shirt are cut off at the shoulders. His frayed denim shorts barely cover his crotch. I try not to stare, but I can't stop looking at his arms.

"Gaetan, this is my nephew, Tom. Tom, this is my roommate Gaetan," Uncle Fred says. "Tom was just about to tell me why he's here and not in Mississauga."

"Do you need a reason?" Gaetan says, with a thick French Canadian accent.

Uncle Fred scowls at Gaetan and nods for me to continue.

"I didn't plan to do it. It just happened. I got in my car to go to work. I pressed play on the cassette player, but instead

13

of "Faith" by George Michael, it was the Village People. "Macho Man." Mom must have used my car before I woke up and left it in the player. It's not the first time."

"That doesn't explain how you got to the airport," Uncle Fred says.

"I forgot how fun the songs were — 'YMCA,' 'In the Navy,'" I tell them. "But there was this one song by them I'd never heard before. It spoke to me. Choked me up, like when you hear the national anthem. It had a choir. The lyrics were all about unity and peace and love. It was about the future and possibilities. And it kept telling me to do one thing over and over again."

"Go West," Gaetan says, like it's the answer on a game show.

"You spent hundreds of dollars and flew across Canada without telling anyone because of 'Go West' by the Village People?" Uncle Fred asks.

"That's the short answer," I tell him.

"You know what that is?" Gaetan says. "That's the power of disco."

Granville Street

I have to resist the urge to take Tom by the hand. I can see he's tired from his flight and the fear of not knowing where he is. We stop in front of a white picket fence, its pointy ends coming up to my nipples, paint peeling in places. It reminds me of the house from *The Waltons*

— two floors with an attic space, a pair of windows popping out of the slanted roof. Each floor has an awning, making the house look tiered, like a wedding cake. The rocking chair on the covered front porch would make the perfect perch for a granny with a gun.

"This is it," I tell Tom. "I've always wondered what it's like inside."

"What did you say your name was again?" he asks.

Seriously, dude? I literally just told him, like, two blocks ago.

"Dwayne," I say. "I should get to work before I'm late. My manager can be a hard ass. He has a total crush on me."

I dig through the cassettes in my canvas satchel and pull out a copy of *Interview with the Vampire* and a pen. I scribble my number on the back page of the book, rip it out, and hand it to Tom.

"Call me," I say.

I continue walking down a street acting cool when really I'm shaking in my Doc Martens. I look back and wave goodbye. Tom has already walked through the gate and doesn't see. I try not to take it personally, but it stings. I still feel like a Good Samaritan even if my motives were selfish. And even if Tom never calls me, he knows I exist. If nothing else, meeting Tom is a distraction from the way my phone call with Warren ended before I left work. Maybe Tom was sent here to replace Warren.

A woman in a tartan jacket with red hair approaches me on Granville Street.

"Excuse me," she says with an Irish accent.

"Yes?" I say, realizing what's she's going to ask as soon as I open my mouth.

"Do you have twenty-five cents?"

"No," I tell her. I always fall for it — she looks too put together to be a panhandler.

I pause in front of the window in Fluevog. The black Munster platform heels Madonna wore to the premier of *Dick Tracy* are proudly displayed in the window next to a framed photo of her wearing them. Makes me proud to be a Canadian. The shop door swings open.

"You!" the store manager yells. He's bald and muscular and wearing a gorgeous pair of two-toned shoes I can't afford. "How many times do I have to tell you to stop fogging up my window?"

"It's not your window," I tell him.

"I'm in charge of it!"

"You couldn't afford those shoes without your employee discount," I say, attempting shade.

"You couldn't afford them *with* my discount. Now run along!"

"Why are you so mean to me?" I practically plead with him. "I'm just like you."

"I am *nothing* like you!" he says and storms back into the store.

What is it about me that makes people think they can be mean to me?

* * *

I see the purple exterior of A&B Sound as I round the corner onto Seymour Street. I still pinch myself every time I walk through the glass door with its brown metal bars, past the high-end stereos, and into the popular music section. Working in a record store was always my dream job. Working at A&B Sound was beyond my wildest expectations.

"Dwayne! What did I say about being late?"

It's my manager, Justice. So much for living the fantasy.

"I got delayed giving a tourist directions," I say.

"Baloney. You got into a fight with the manager at Fluevog again," Justice says.

"Lies! How dare you!"

Justice is a Goth. He tones it down at work but I ran into him that one time I snuck into the Luvaffair and he was full on Robert Smith from The Cure. He bosses me around as an excuse to talk to me. He's still nicer to me than most people. And I do owe him my job.

Every "cool" kid at school applied expecting to get hired like it was owed to them. What they didn't expect was Justice. There were two parts to the job interview. First, I had to name the album and artist based on a cryptic description, snippets of melodies, music videos, and album covers. Then I had to make music recommendations based on another album. I'd been preparing for this interview my entire life without even knowing it. There was a method to Justice's madness. All I do all shift long is tell people the albums they're describing or suggest an album based on something they already like.

"Get punched in," Justice says. "The floor needs restocking."

I run up the stairs to the Classical, Jazz, and Country sections. I see my friend Raven's pompadour and tattoos as she flips through the cassettes. Raven DJs at the Lotus and Ms. Ts. I always sneak her promotional copies of albums. She's, like, the coolest person that comes into this place.

"Hey, Raven. What are you doing in Country?"

"Replacing Gina's copy of *Absolute Torch and Twang* for her birthday," she says, holding up the tape. "Hers is so stretched, it sounds like Wagner."

"Isn't that album, like, a year old now?"

"As long as it's not 'Closer to Fine,'" Raven sighs. "If one more person requests that song…"

"Come with me to the back. There's a new album I think you'll like," I tell her.

I go into the storeroom and return with an album stamped "Promotional Copy." The cover is psychedelic-looking. Three people, two guys and girl, are posing in a field of stars with seventies-style daisies on the edges. The woman's wearing Fluevogs.

"They're the B-52's but funkier," I tell her. "Track nine is going to be the song of the summer."

"Deee-Lite. I've heard of them," Raven says, staring at the sleeve. "Are you sure you don't mind giving this to me?"

"The cassette is in my Walkman as we speak."

"I need to get a cake for Gina and drop it off at Fred's," Raven says. "We're having a birthday party for her later. You should drop by after work if you're not busy."

"At the green house on Bute?"

"That's the one."

Bute Street

Uncle Fred's room is painted white. I'm wrapped in white sheets. The sun against the white curtains reminds me of light projected onto a movie screen. There's not a thing out of place. The furniture looks handmade by Quakers except for a red trunk decorated with flowers like the tickle trunk on *Mr. Dressup*.

I rub the sleep from my eyes and plant my bare feet on the hardwood floor. I go to the dresser and look at the framed photos. Fred and a woman with an Elvis haircut posing with hand puppets. Fred naked on a beach, smiling, his arm draped over the shoulder of another naked man with a moustache. A woman with long blonde hair and a guitar performing at a bar. Funny. The woman could pass for my aunt if I had one. There's not a single photo of our family. Like we don't exist.

At the top of the stairs, I hear my uncle and Gaetan talking in the living room over the whoosh-whoosh of fans.

"That doesn't mean a thing," Uncle Fred says.

"How many straight guys fly across the country because of the Village People?" Gaetan asks him.

"My brother likes the Village People and he's the straightest guy I know," Fred says.

"If your nephew's not gay, he's questioning," Gaetan says.

"THAT'S IT!" I shout. I run down the stairs and into the living room. "Questioning! That's exactly what I am!"

Gaetan is sprawled on the couch in front of a large square fan. Fred is reclining in a La-Z-Boy chair, another fan pointed up his shorts.

"Were you listening in on our conversation?" Uncle Fred asks. "Because that's not an attractive way to repay your host."

"Not on purpose," I say. "Gaetan hit it perfectly on the nose. I never heard it described like that."

"Because they don't teach it in school," Gaetan says.

"Now that we have that resolved," Uncle Fred says. "I spoke with your parents while you were asleep."

"How'd it go?" I ask.

"I preferred it when all we talked about was the weather," Fred says. "I called them at the right time. They were just starting to get worried."

"Was Dad angry?"

"Your dad doesn't get angry, he gets quiet," Uncle Fred says.

"Sorry Uncle Fred."

"It wasn't nearly as bad as the time I scored on myself in soccer the summer of '76," Fred says, waving the conversation away. "I convinced him to let you stay here until you're ready to go home on the condition you call them first thing in the morning."

"I promise."

"There's something I need to tell you. Vancouver is hosting the Gay Games in a week. We're billeting an athlete, so you'll be sleeping with me in my room a bit longer. I should warn you, it's going to be all gay all the time around here."

"I know about the Gay Games," I tell him.

"You do?"

"I took a pamphlet when I went to the Youth Drop-In at The 519."

"You've went to the gay community centre in Toronto?" Uncle Fred gets out of his recliner and hugs me. "I thought you were getting back at your dad for something. You really are questioning."

"Yeah. I am."

"Lucky you. For eight days you're going to experience what it would be like if gays ran the world."

"That reminds me," Gaetan says. "I need to stock up on condoms before they run out at Shoppers Drug Mart on Davie."

"What time is it?" I ask. "How long have I been asleep?"

"A few hours," Uncle Fred says. "Company is coming."

* * *

"Hey Fred!" a voice calls out from the front door.

"We're back here!" Uncle Fred shouts through the open back door. He's stretched out on a lawn chair enjoying the orange sky. Gaetan is lying on a blanket next to him.

The woman from the photo, the one with the Elvis haircut and tattoos, comes outside. She's brought a friend. A younger woman, about my age. Her hair is tied back with a red bandana. She looks like she could be a mechanic.

"Hey Raven, I'd like you to meet my nephew Tom," Fred says. "The Village People sent him here from Mississauga."

"The Goddess works in mysterious ways," Raven says, planting her palm into mine. "Tom, this is Gina."

"Hey," Gina says, raising two fingers in the peace sign.

I don't know who Gina is, but she's already the coolest girl I've ever met.

"We were in the hood and thought we'd drop by," Raven says.

"We weren't anywhere near here," Gina corrects.

"I'm going to go to the gym," Gaetan says. "I need to perk up my tits before my shift at the bar."

"Mind if I grab a beer from the fridge?" Raven asks.

"Go for it. I'll go inside with you," says Fred. "I want to put some aloe on my skin."

Everyone goes back into the house except Gina. Why do I get the feeling the adults left us alone so the two of us can "rap" like a very special episode of *Facts of Life*?

"So how does Raven know my uncle?" I ask her.

Gina's face lights up.

"Crazy story," she says. "They used to be puppeteers together."

"What? *She* was a puppeteer? For kids?"

"I know! It's crazy, right? They used to travel all over the country working for this Christian couple. They had a TV show in Alberta and everything. It's like they were in some sort of cult."

Gina takes a seat next to me in Uncle Fred's lawn chair. I feel like I've passed some sort of test.

"You close to your uncle?" she asks.

"Not really," I say. "Not at all. My family almost never talks about him."

23

"Too bad for them. Even the dykes on The Drive like Fred. Most of them don't even like each other. How long does it take to get a beer?"

The back door opens. We both look, expecting Fred and Raven. A lanky guy dressed in black steps outside. It's Dwayne. The guy who gave me directions this afternoon.

"Hey Dwayne!" Gina says.

"You know Dwayne?" I ask.

"He's Raven's inside man at A&B Sound."

"Hey Gina," Dwayne says. "I hope you don't mind that I dropped by for your birthday party. Raven said I should come by after work."

"What birthday party?" Gina asks.

The back door opens. Raven is holding a cake glowing with candles. Raven, Fred, and Gaetan start singing "Happy Birthday." Gina looks over at me as I sing along as well.

"Did you know about this?" she asks me. I nod my head yes.

"Make a wish and blow out the candles," Fred says. "But don't tell us what you wish for."

Gina takes a deep breath and blows out eighteen candles in one breath. I don't know what she wished for, but I wish that every day could feel like this.

Sunday, July 29, 1990

Bute Street

I'm woken up by the smell of fresh brewed coffee and toast. I follow my nose down the stairs to the kitchen. Uncle Fred is sitting at the table reading the *Vancouver Sun*, a plate of toast smothered in marmalade within his reach.

"Help yourself to anything," Fred says without looking up from the paper. "Except the Pop Tarts. Gaetan will kill you if you eat his Pop Tarts."

"Is Gaetan still asleep?"

"Probably at the tubs."

"The bathroom was empty when I came downstairs," I say.

"Not that kind of tub," Fred says.

I go to pour myself a glass of orange juice and notice a full-page newspaper ad on the refrigerator door. An illustration of an hourglass fills the page with the ominous warning, "Time is running out for the impending Sodomite Invasion."

"What's this all about?" I ask.

"That's what happens when churches don't pay taxes," Fred says. "It's Pastor Robert Birch and the Burnaby Christian Fellowship. They've been having prayer meetings twice a month to stop the Games. They're convinced a pox will be cast upon our houses if the Games go on."

"That's super intense."

"It backfired. That ad increased public support for the Games. The organizers even fundraised off it. They made these cute shirts that say 'Time is running out to donate to the Games.' People came out of the woodwork to volunteer."

The ad makes me shudder. It takes a lot of hate to put an ad like that in the paper. It's what keeps me from dealing with these ... feelings ... I keep having. I don't know how Uncle Fred is able to keep the ad on the fridge.

"I need to get my butt to the pool and train," Fred says. "The swimming competition will be here before I know it."

"*You're* competing in the Games?"

"Try not to sound so shocked," he says.

"You don't strike me as athletic."

"I'm not. I'm using the Games to conquer my fear of competition."

"Don't you have to qualify first?"

"Anybody can participate in the Games regardless of age, gender, sexuality, or skill level," Uncle Fred says.

"I don't know why we invite straight people to our Games when they won't let us play in theirs," says Gaetan, entering the kitchen. He smells like chlorine. Has he been swimming?

"I think you just answered your own question," Fred says.

"Can I come to the pool?" I ask.

"You need to call you parents."

"I'm really fast at the breast stroke. I can coach you."

"Why did I think you played water polo?" Uncle Fred asks.

"I do. But I still know how to do all the strokes."

"Do you now?" Gaetan says, raising his eyebrows.

Uncle Fred thinks about it.

"As long as you don't yell at me to go faster," he says. "And promise to call your parents when you get home."

"Promise. Do either of you have a bathing suit I can borrow?

"I have just the thing," Gaetan says. "Follow me."

Pacific Street

I look to my poster of Madonna for spiritual guidance. My hand hovers above the Princess phone on my night table. I should know better than to call Tom this early in the morning. This is what got me in trouble with Warren. I punch the numbers into the phone fast as I can. Tom's uncle answers just as I'm about to hang up.

"Hey Uncle Fred," I say into the phone. "It's Dwayne, Raven's friend. I was wondering … is Tom awake?"

"You can just call me Fred, and yes. Tom's awake," he says before shouting, "Tom! It's your friend Dwayne."

He called me Tom's friend!

"Hey Dwayne, what's up?" Tom says into the phone.

"I'm registering volunteers for the Games," I say casually. "But I'm free after if you want to do something later today."

"Maybe. I need to call my parents at some point," he groans.

"Good luck with that," I say. "I'll be at the West End Community Centre on Denman if you want some moral support."

"Sounds good. I'll catch up with you later."

Will he? Or is Tom just saying that to be polite? Three quick knocks rattle my bedroom door. Mom pokes her head in.

"Dwayne! Walk me to work," she orders.

Me and Mom live in a townhouse on the corner of Bute and Pacific. Mom moved in with her gay best friend, Gregory, after her parents kicked her out when she got pregnant with me. Gregory was the reason mom became a nurse. She used to party with Gregory and his friends. When they started getting sick with AIDS, she went to nursing school so they'd have a friend at the hospital. She's been working on 10-C, the AIDS ward at St. Paul's Hospital, ever since.

Mom took over the lease after Gregory died. Even with the rent hikes, we still pay less than a one-bedroom in the Vaseline Towers on Burnaby Street. It's not a house, but it's not an apartment either. I had a backyard growing up. That's a luxury when you live in a city.

"I'm worried about you volunteering at the Gay Games," Mom says, huffing her way up the hill on Bute in her nurse's uniform.

"Excuse me? You were the one who encouraged me to volunteer."

I was against it at first. Why should I celebrate a community that doesn't even see me unless I go to the gym five hundred hours a week? Then I agreed to give it a try. I'm glad I did. I volunteer mostly at the Gay Games office at The Centre at Bute and Davie. I've put together boxes of Gay Games pamphlets and t-shirts for the drag queens to take to the balls; for the leathermen to take to Mr. Leather events; and for the jocks to take to tournaments to promote the Games all over the world. I've seen with my own eyes the outpouring of support from people from around the globe. Letters of encouragement. Dollar donations in every currency wishing us a great

Games. I've entered a registration form for an athlete in Russia into a computer. Mary Brookes, the office manager, is always reminding me, "We are putting on the Olympics with spare change and pocket lint."

"I still think it's important you see there's more to being gay than discos and bars," Mom says. "But I want you to be careful. My friend in ER says there's been more bashing the closer we get to the Games."

"I promise to be careful," I say, kissing her on the forehead when we get to Bute and Nelson. We part ways. Mom turns right to go to St. Paul's, and I turn left toward the Community Centre.

Quelle surprise. The born-again crazies are protesting in front of the West End Community Centre. Cardboard signs bob up and down like ducks on the ocean. Bible verses taken out of context so that they conform to their narrow points of view. The old woman with the sandwich board is there. I want to tell them their poor penmanship offends me, but I can't afford a black eye this close to Opening Ceremonies. I turn up Deee-Lite on my Walkman to drown out the chants of "Sinner! Pervert! Repent!"

The auditorium has been converted into a circuit of foldout tables and scrims. Paper arrows point the way. I follow the twists and turns up to the stage to where Heather, the volunteer coordinator, is assigning jobs.

"Hey, Dwayne, I hope the protestors didn't bother you too much," Heather says.

"What's a little damnation before lunch?" I say with a shrug.

"There's the spirit!" Heather runs down the clipboard with her pen searching for my name. "I have you at the new registrant table."

"Point the way."

Heather uses her pen to point to a foldout table near the entrance. I smile at the other volunteers as I make my way to my station. I take my seat at the table. I can see the protestors on the sidewalk through the open doors. One makes eye contact with me. I glare at him until he looks away.

Bute Street

I get off the phone with Dwayne and run up the stairs to Gaetan's room. The bed is unmade and there's clothes everywhere. Mom would lose it if she saw my room like this. A pair of Speedos hit me in the face. Then a pair of frayed shorts bounce off my chest. A sleeveless plaid shirt is draped over my head like I'm a chair.

"Those are my lucky shorts," Gaetan says. "I always get laid in those."

"I'm not trying to get laid," I tell him.

"Everyone is trying to get laid, even when they're not," he says. "Go ahead. Try them on."

"With you watching?"

"You're a jock. You've changed in front of other boys before."

I eye Gaetan like he's trying to trick me into something.

"Get over yourself, girl," he says sharply, his English crossing over into French. "I'm into bears, not trade."

"Did you just call me a girl? And what's trade?"

"Put on the outfit. I need to go to sleep."

I shuck my jeans to the floor. Gaetan whistles. I cover myself with my hands and give him a look.

"I'm kidding," he says.

I can tell by looking at him that Gaetan doesn't see me as someone to sleep with but as someone to look out for. I've never felt that from another guy. Not outside of sports, anyway.

"How did you end up living with my uncle?" I ask him. "You two don't seem anything alike."

"He was my lawyer. I used to hustle the neighbourhood."

"Like a pool shark?"

"Like a prostitute," he laughs. "This area used to be crawling with them. That's why there are so many one-way streets in the West End."

"This neighbourhood?"

"Didn't you see that documentary, *Hookers on Davie*?" Gaetan says. "The city cracked down on us for Expo '86. Your uncle kept a lot of us out of jail. Free of charge."

I zip up the fly on the denim shorts and slip my arms through the holes in the plaid shirt where the sleeves used to be.

"What do you think?" I ask.

"You should go to the Dufferin," Gaetan says. "You won't pay for a drink until you're thirty. Now get out. I can feel the bags under my eyes."

Uncle Fred is waiting for me at the bottom of the stairs.

"You look like you escaped from *Petticoat Junction*," he says.

Uncle Fred opens the front door. The hallway fills with sunlight like that closet in *Poltergeist*. I put my aviators on like Tom Cruise in *Top Gun*. Fred's flip-flops slap the porch steps and as he goes down them. He holds the front gate open for me. I have a flashback to when I was a kid. I don't remember the time or the place but this feels familiar, like we've done this before. It's the most relaxed I've felt in weeks.

Brockton Oval

"Hey, Gina!" Rhonda, my coach, shouts to me as she unlocks the equipment box behind home plate.

"Hey, Rhonda!" I shout back, as I approach Brockton Oval on my bike.

Today is our last chance to practice as a team before the Games. I volunteered to help set up the diamond to avoid looking at mom while she was getting ready for church. I thought Brockton Oval would be shadier, since it's surrounded by the trees in Stanley Park. No such luck.

Raven is waving her arms at me as I ride past the bike rack.

"I didn't expect to see you here this early on a Sunday morning after a night of spinning," I tell Raven while I lock up my bike.

"Believe me, Baby Girl, I'd still be in bed if I didn't have something to tell you."

I love it/hate it that she calls me Baby Girl. It makes me feel naive and protected at the same time.

Raven and I met the night I snuck into The Lotus. I must have looked like a deer in headlights because Raven spotted me from the DJ booth and invited me up. She told me who to look out for and who I should get to know. At the end of the night, she gave me a lift home in her Camaro, but instead of kissing me goodnight, she asked, "Have you ever played softball?"

"I have something to tell you," Raven says, shading her eyes from the sun.

"Timbre and Cerise are moving in together?" I ask. Timbre is my first ex-girlfriend. Cerise plays second for our team. They hooked up at one of our team barbecues not long after I came out to my parents.

"Give it a week," Raven says. "I just wanted to let you know I ran into Timbre's friend Tiffany last night at the bar."

"I can't stand Tiffany. She is so waiting for Timbre to tell her she's been in love with her all along."

"You're going to hate her more after you hear this," Raven says. "Turns out Timbre has been telling her groupies you're the one who dumped her because you're in love with me."

"I thought she was playing at some Women's Festival," I say. "How does she have the time to be spreading rumours about me?"

"She's a lesbian folk singer," Raven says. "She's got her finger on the pulse of every lesbian coffee shop between here and Portland."

"One moment please," I say, holding up a finger.

I walk out into the outfield and scream for a full two minutes.

"You okay?" Rhonda shouts. She's painting the baselines, a cigarette hanging between her lips. I give her a thumbs up as I walk back toward Raven.

"Do people believe her?" I ask Raven.

"Timbre has a gravelly voice and a guitar. Of course they do."

"I'll never be able to walk down The Drive again. Cheating on Timbre is like Cheating on Melissa Etheridge with one of the Indigo Girls. No one will take my side."

"It's gossip. It'll blow over."

"Blow over? The Games are in a week! Do you know how hard it's been to concentrate on my game knowing she's sleeping with second base? Do you know how many times I've wanted to aim the ball at Cerice's shin instead of her glove?"

"That's why I'm telling you this now, so you won't do that in a game," Raven says. "We have a shot at a medal!"

"Why is Timbre doing this? She got what she wanted. She's already dragged my heart through the mud. Now she has to make *me* the villain?"

Raven puts her tattooed arm around my shoulder and says, "The thing you have to remember about Timbre is she needs to be the star of the show. Timbre broke up with you because you're playing in the Gay Games."

"So is Timbre. She has a spot in the GAYLA, the celebration of women's culture."

"But you're stealing focus," Raven explains. "This whole thing between you, her, and Cerise is about keeping the spotlight on Timbre. Don't let her do that. Don't let her ruin your Games. Trust me on this."

Everything Raven is saying makes so much sense. So why am I still so angry?

"Are you to going to pitch in or gossip all morning?" Rhonda shouts. "Those bases aren't going to hammer themselves into the ground."

Second Beach Pool

Uncle Fred's head bobs up and down in the water as he paddles toward me. The water is as warm as the air. It's crystal clear against the blue cement of the pool. It reminds me of the bacta tank from *The Empire Strikes Back*. The sun casts honeycombs of light on the pool floor. The black line down the centre of the slow lane looks staticky through the water's surface. A little old lady passes Fred.

"How did I do?" he asks me when he touches the wall.

"Three minutes, thirty seconds," I tell him.

"I'm getting faster!" he says, delighted.

"I can swim a hundred metres in under two minutes," I say.

"You're young. You have hormones on top of hormones," he says. "I need to stretch to get out of bed. The only reason I'm doing the breast stroke is because it's the closest thing to the dog paddle."

"If you'd just do what I told you and put your heels together before you kick you'd go so much farther," I tell him.

"You sound like your father."

"Don't you want to win a medal?"

"I want to finish," Fred says. "And I plan on raising my arms in victory no matter what place I come in."

"I thought you wanted to get over your fear of competition."

"I do."

"Competition isn't about swimming in a race. It's swimming for gold."

"You make it sound like I'm mocking the Games."

"All I'm saying is you have to be in it to win it or there's no point in participating."

My uncle takes this in. I think I've lit a fire under his ass but he says, "I need a break."

"You've only swam three hundred metres."

"What did I say about telling me to go faster?"

Uncle Fred glides over to the ladder and pulls himself out of the water. He's wearing the tiniest speedo I've ever seen. His skin is white and freckled. His legs are as thick as his arms. We stretch out on our towels on the cement deck. Fred's eyes drift toward the aquafitness instructor whose movements are being imitated by a pool full of seniors in floppy hats and sunglasses.

"So what are you planning on telling your parents when you talk to them?" Uncle Fred asks.

"Don't know."

"Does your dad have any idea you're *questioning*?" Uncle Fred puts air quotes around the word.

"I don't think so. He says things though. Like ... one time we were watching a re-run of *Three's Company* and Jack was acting gay for Mr. Roper, and Dad said, 'I'll send you to military school if I ever catch you acting like that.' He keeps making these hints about how upset he would be if I were anything but straight."

"I wonder if that has something to do with living with me," Fred wonders. "You said yesterday you went to The 519. So you know where the bars are in Toronto.

Have you kissed a boy?"

"I haven't done anything. With anyone. But I want to. It's just all so unfamiliar to me. When I saw the pamphlet for the Gay Games I thought, *I know about sports. I can relate to sports.* I tried to come up with excuses to tell my parents for visiting you, but I knew dad wouldn't let me. That's why I ran away."

"I thought it was the Village People."

"They gave me the push I needed."

"If sports is what brought you here, sports is why you're going to volunteer for the Games."

"Say what?"

"You heard me. If you're going to stay at my house, you have to volunteer for the Games."

"But I'm not gay."

"No, but you're questioning, and that counts." Fred gets up from his towel. "Now let's get back in the pool. I want you to teach me how to pace myself so I have enough energy for the home stretch. I don't care which place I finish, as long as I finish strong."

Uncle Fred walks into the pool, barely making a splash as he disappears below the surface of the water.

Brockton Oval

Cerise has been stuck on second for a couple of runners now. Rhonda walks up to the plate. There's two out. The first pitch is a ball. Raven gets a clap going in the dugout. My heart isn't in it. It's on second base. Squished between Cerise's cleat and the base pad.

What was Cerise thinking when she took up with Timbre? We're on the same team! We're supposed to support each other on and off the field, not steal our girlfriends. And if Cerise had been in love with Timbre for years like she told Rhonda, who told Raven, who told me, why couldn't she have waited until after the Gay Games? Another two weeks wasn't going to kill her!

I was the last to know. I went to Josephine's, played ball, and partied. All of Timbre's friends knew she was seeing Cerise behind my back. They smiled at me and said nothing. Except for Tiffany and Lorna or Tweedle-Dum and Tweedle-Dee, as I call them. They'd feed me breadcrumbs. Ask where Timbre was if I was out alone. Pretend to be interested in Cerise. Raven told me before Timbre did.

"This is why I live in the West End," Raven explained when she told me about Timbre and Cerise. "The Drive is too incestuous. These two start dating, they break up and date other people, then they have affairs with their ex's ex, and so on and so on. Charles and Diana have nothing on us."

Raven warned me about Timbre. Rhonda too. But how can you say no when the most famous lesbian in Vancouver only has eyes for you? She sang love songs directly to me at her shows. It was magical. Like Cinderella, but with key rings and army boots.

I can't let Timbre ruin my Games. I can't let any woman ruin my Games. I will focus on fast-pitch and fast-pitch only. I will use the Games to put Timbre behind me.

Crack!

Rhonda hits a line drive between second and third. She gets to first. Cerise is stopped at third.

"Gina! You're up!" Raven calls. Raven slaps my ass as I leave the dugout to grab a bat and jog to the plate. "Hit it out of the park, Baby Girl."

I hold up my hand to the pitcher to give me a moment to find my stance. I lock eyes with her and wait for the pitch. I can see Cerise out of the corner of my eye. Her mind is clearly on the Game. I hate her for that.

"Strike!"

I take a step back, breathe, and take my stance. The pitch comes and I swing. There's a lot of things I'm not good at. I can't sew a button to save my life. I can't boil an egg without the shell sticking to the white. But at the deli counter where I work, I can slice a hundred grams of cold cuts without weighing it. And I know how to hit a ball. Cerise can steal my girlfriend, but I refuse to let her steal something that comes so naturally to me. I step back up to the plate.

CLUNK!

It's the same sound a pinball machine makes when you win a free game. The sound a tongue makes when it's clucked against the top of your mouth, but louder. I watch as the outfield goes in hot pursuit of the ball. Cerise crosses home plate. Rhonda looks like she's going to have a heart attack as she rounds third base. Cheers from the dugout get louder. The ball is being thrown infield. Second base jumps to catch it but the ball grazes the tip of her glove. The pitcher runs to pick up the ball. It's too late. I'm already home.

Cerise raises her hand in a high-five. I return it instinctively. It's like we both forgot who we were high-fiving. I will put her out of my mind. I don't have to like Cerise. I just have to play ball with her.

Denman Street

"Dwayne, what are you still doing here?" Heather says when she sees me at the table. "You should have gone home by now."

The clock on the wall is pointing to four. My volunteer shift was over at two. But everyone has been so nice. I've made small talk with people I would have never met if it wasn't for the Games. I'm a cynic. I think people are naturally mean. That's been my experience, anyway. But I'm starting to wonder if all the assholes in the world are distracting us from all the nice people.

"Scoot!" Heathers says. "Save your energy for the athlete's registration."

I give her a limp-wristed salute. I notice my shoe is

untied as I push my chair from the folding table. As I bend over to tie my laces, I hear a cartoonish woman's voice say, "Excuse me? Is this where I register to be a volunteer?"

It's Tom. He's dressed like one of Madonna's back-up dancers. From boy scout to go-go dancer in less than forty-eight hours. That has to be a record. His aviator glasses hang from the top button of his shirt, pulling it down so I can see the top of his chest. He's probably seen *Top Gun* ten times. I'd bet a hundred dollars there's a copy of George Michael's *Faith* hidden in his room.

"I'm done for the day," I tell him.

"Please register me," Tom says with a smile. "You're my first friend in Vancouver."

I wonder if Tom can turn the charm on and off or if it comes naturally to him. The way he is looking at me now, he could tell me to jump off the Lions Gate Bridge and I'd do it.

"Well if you can't be an athlete, be an athletic supporter," I say, sliding a registration form across the table, along with a pen. If Tom has seen *Grease*, he doesn't know its most famous joke. "Did you catch the Gay Games spirit?"

"Uncle Fred wants me to experience what it'd be like if gays ruled the world."

"What do you think so far?"

"I could live without the protestors."

I go with Tom to get his volunteer ID badge. His photo

43

looks like it was taken at Andy Warhol's factory. Mine looks like it was taken in a bowling alley photo booth.

"You can take the bus and SkyTrain for free with that thing," I tell him, pointing to his badge.

"Cool!'

I have to look away when he smiles. I don't want him to know how attracted I am to him. I don't want to scare him off. I can be Tom's best friend if I play it cool. Until he realizes how much he loves me.

"I can arrange for us to be partners at the athlete's registration on Wednesday," I tell him. "If you want."

"I'd like that," he says. "What're you doing now? Want to hang out?"

It's been months since someone asked me that.

"I know a beach where the locals go," I say.

"Lead the way."

We cross Denman Street and walk toward Stanley Park. The West End is pretty nice as far as neighbourhoods go, but west of Denman is nicer. It's where the rich kids at school live. Lots of old money. "Newly wed or nearly dead," is how Mom describes it.

"That voice you used at registration," I say. "Do you use that when you're making fun of the fags at school?"

Tom looks ahead like he has blinders on. It's the first time he's stopped smiling since he showed up at the community centre.

"Now that you mention it, I guess I have," he says.

"You know how it is. Just behaving like one of the guys so no one suspects what's really going on."

"I've heard that voice a lot at school," I tell him. "If you're going to be a volunteer for the Games I suggest you put that voice away for a while."

"Got it," he says. "I'm surprised to hear you get teased at school."

"Because I'm such a jock?"

"No. Because everyone here is so …"

"Gay?"

"Yeah."

We turn left at Chilco. I can see the ocean glittering like sequins between the trees at the end of the street.

"People aren't out at school. Not on purpose, anyway."

"I still think it would be cool to grow up here. The ocean right at your doorstep. Every type of person."

"I remember seeing your uncle's roommate working the streets when I walked to elementary school."

"Gaetan? Really?"

"I was so in love with him," I say.

"I'm telling him you said that."

"Don't!" I slap his arm as a joke, but also as an excuse to touch him. He doesn't flinch.

I want to tell Tom I've also seen guys not much older than we are pushed around in wheel chairs like old men. But I don't want to scare him back into the closet.

I lead Tom down some cement stairs to a small lagoon

bordered by rocks. The tide is coming in. Heads bob on the surface of the ocean like apples. Someone is softly playing a guitar. Someone else is smoking a joint. We take off our shoes and find a log to lean against. We watch the simmering sun take its time setting. When it finally disappears behind the mountains, Tom says, "You will always be safe as long as I'm around."

His words hang there. I don't know if he feels bad because I called him on his shit, but he seems sincere. I don't need his protection. But it's nice to know it's there.

Wednesday, August 1, 1990
Athlete's Registration

Denman Street

"Have you seen this?" Dwayne asks. He flops a copy of *The Province* on the table next to the camera. The paper is opened to the Opinions page. The headline reads, "Gay Games: More Than Physical Muscle Being Flexed."

"Uncle Fred read it out loud last night at dinner," I tell him. "He couldn't believe his eyes."

"Neither could I when Mary showed it to me just now," Dwayne says. "For four years, these guys did nothing but ridicule the Games. They went so far as to publish a full-page ad threatening us with the wrath of God. Now they're telling everyone to come and have a good time."

"They must have figured out how much money the city is going to make from the athletes," says a volunteer at the station next to ours.

We're waiting for the first athletes to walk through the gymnasium doors. They will arrive by the busload, we were told, driven here from the airport by more volunteers. They will leave here with their ID badge, which gets them on the bus and the SkyTrain for free, a map of the city, passes to social events for the athletes, the official program, and learn who their billet is. Dwayne managed to convince the volunteer coordinator into letting us take the ID photos.

"Not only will we be taking pictures of some of the hottest gay athletes in the world, but we get to talk to them too!" Dwayne said when I arrived for my volunteer shift.

It's a hundred degrees outside. Except for his blue volunteer shirt, Dwayne is dressed all in black. Meanwhile, I can feel sweat rolling down my spine to the crack of my ass.

"Have you called your parents yet?" Dwayne asks, killing time.

"Not yet."

"Does your uncle know?"

"Not yet."

"Aren't you worried they're to call *you* if you keep putting it off?" Dwayne asks.

"A little bit. My parents aren't ones to discuss feelings. Especially my dad. He's more of a keep-your-emotions-to-yourself kind of guy."

"Sounds healthy," Dwayne says.

"Don't get me wrong," I say. "Dad is great. He'd do anything for me. When I wanted to play water polo he found a team I could play on and went out of his way to drive me there. He coached my softball team and encouraged me to learn to become an umpire. I don't want to disappoint him."

"I still don't get why you left the way you did. And drop the crap about the Village People. I love a well-choreographed number as much as the next guy, but no one spends a thousand bucks on airfare because of 'YMCA.'"

"It was 'Go West,' and it was only five hundred dollars. The agent at the gate said Air Canada was offering a special rate for the Gay Games."

"Whatever."

Dwayne rolls his eyes and punches me lightly on the shoulder. He's trying to pass it off as a friendly tap, but I've been hit on by drunk girls at parties enough times to know he's looking for an excuse to touch me.

Mary, the short woman with the English accent, takes the microphone and says, "The first bus of athletes has just left the airport."

The volunteers cheer. The auditorium crackles with excitement like a homecoming game. The volunteer

49

coordinators run us through the registration process one last time. Everyone is giddy like we're waiting for the guest of honour at a surprise party.

"My hands, they're shaking," Dwayne says. He holds them up for me to see. "It's happening. They're coming! Can you believe it? How do I look?"

He's behaving like a housewife preparing a dinner for her husband's boss. I've only known Dwayne for a couple of days, but I've noticed he tries to come off as indifferent and above it all. It's kind of cute to see him this excited.

"Can I get you some water?" I ask him.

"Did I get weird? I get anxious sometimes. I've actually never told anyone that. Why am I still talking?"

"It must be the heat."

Dwayne looks at me with a puppy dog smile. He has a nice smile. He should use it more often. And maybe stop dressing like Morticia Addams.

Third Avenue

Mom is waiting to get into the bathroom when I come out wrapped in a towel. My skin is already warming up after my cold shower. I smell like green apple soap from The Body Shop. My hair is wet and hanging down to my shoulders.

"Gina, you look so pretty," Mom says when she sees me. "Why can't you look like this all the time?"

"Naked in a towel?" I ask. "I'd get arrested."

50

"This," she says, holding my hair in clumps like cooked spaghetti. "You have such beautiful hair and you hide it with that bandana. Men go crazy for this."

I can't be bothered to argue with her. I sigh and go back to my room. The clothes I'm going to wear to registration are carefully laid out on my bed. My favourite black T-shirt — ironed, of course. My perfectly frayed denim shorts. And my Nikes, which I have scrubbed back to their original white. If I'm going to be an ambassador to the city I might as well look good.

Mom *tsks* at how I'm dressed when I go out into the living room. Her tsk is the product of eighteen years of disappointments. And each *tsk* stings like the very first one.

"I wish you would stop with this ... Games ..." She can't bring herself to say the word *gay*.

"Why can't you just be happy for me?" I say. "Everyone at the deli is and they're as Old World as you. Even *The Province* gave the Gay Games its seal of approval."

"All the newspaper wants is your money. I want what's best for you."

"Then you should be happy I'm good at something! I could be pregnant. I could be on drugs. I could be in jail. Instead I'm a lesbian softball player. This as a win, Ma!"

Mom throws up her hands and walks off to the kitchen. I don't know how I can make it any plainer for her to understand. We've given up on each other. I tie my hair back with my bandana just to bug her. She doesn't say goodbye when I leave.

I roll my shirt sleeves up to my shoulders when I get to Commercial Drive. I hate that I have to turn the corner to change identities. At least Wonder Woman gets to spin around. I can see the 20 Victoria bus stopped on the other side of 1st Avenue. I spare myself some sweat stains and wait for it instead of walking the six blocks to the SkyTrain station.

I sit on the bench, waving my hand in front of my face to cool off. Seven faces look back at me from the Celebration '90 poster in the shelter. Five guys, two women, smiling and harmless. *Come Celebrate with Us*, the poster reads. Raven can't stand the poster. The Gay Games board was offered a 75 percent discount on advertising if they removed the words *Gay* and *Games* from the bus shelter ads; they were afraid they'd be vandalized.

"Come celebrate what?" Raven complained the first time she saw the poster. "If you don't know what Celebration '90 is, then you don't know what the Gay Games are."

"It says Gay Games on the hot guy's tank top," I pointed out to her.

"You kids today," she sighed.

I get Raven's point, but I could also see the board's. Seventy-five percent is a lot of money. That's where Raven and I differ. Raven is a full-on radical dyke. I'm

52

just happy we got the Games. Maybe I've come to expect so little as a gay person that I don't have the guts to ask for more. But I did agree with Raven: it was a shitty thing for the board to force the Queer Arts Festival to remove the word *queer* from its name or lose their Gay Games affiliation. I mean, the posters had already gone out. Come on.

Gay and Queer. Two words for the same thing. One word is offensive to a segment of one population; the other is offensive to another. Doesn't matter which word you use, gay people are still asking permission to exist.

I get off the bus at Commercial Station and wait for the SkyTrain, a leftover from the last time Vancouver welcomed the world. There were no threats of violence and damnation or the fear of AIDS getting spread for Expo '86. They sure as hell didn't have to worry about fundraising and posters. Instead, the car I'm on has a plaque honouring some head of state that rode the train during Expo.

I walk from Burrard Station to Fred's place on Bute Street. Fred opens the door when I arrive.

"Hey, Baby Girl," Fred says when he sees me.

"Are you saying that now too?" I ask him.

"If it looks like a duck and it walks like a duck," he says.

"Are Tom and Dwayne here?"

"They're registering athletes," Fred says. "Don't worry. You'll get to play with Curly and Moe soon."

I look at him like I don't know what he's talking about. But Fred can see right through me. Even I didn't know how much I was looking forward to seeing them until just now.

Denman Street

"Hey, Dwayne, can you grab another roll of film?" Tom asks.

I reach down into the bin next to me and grab another Polaroid cartridge. Up until now, I had assumed the Games were going to be another party for buff white guys. Instead, this is the most Brown and Asian people I've ever seen in the West End since Expo. And some of them are checking me out! But I only have eyes for Tom. As do many of the guys who get their photo taken by him.

"Ta-dah!" Tom says, having loaded the camera.

I promised myself I wouldn't let my feelings for Tom get in the way of our friendship. As Faye Dunaway as Joan Crawford once said, "This ain't my first time at the rodeo." I need to learn how to let things take care of themselves instead of forcing them. If Tom and I are meant to happen, it will happen on its own. That said, I still get jealous whenever some himbo gives Tom a come-hither look.

"How long have we been doing this now?" Tom asks, stretching his back.

"Four hours. Need a neck massage?" Like that didn't sound desperate.

"I'll stretch when we're done."

"Oy!" echoes across our area like a bass drum. I plug my ears. "Oy!"

A tanned hairy man wearing a kangaroo pattern romper with matching socks takes his place in front of the camera. He is vibrating like a guitar string. It's been like this all day. The visiting athletes are like kids at a birthday party who have had way too much cake and ice cream. He steps away from the scrim to shake both mine and Tom's hands vigorously.

"Name's Kouri. I'm a wrestlah," he announces. Then he says to Tom, "Nice shoulders on ya. You a wrestlah?"

"I'm a volunteer, but I play water polo," Tom says.

"Water polo. Good sport that."

"Tom's not gay," I say, worried about where this is going.

"I'm questioning," Tom says.

"Looks like you found your answer," Kouri says, laughing like a pirate.

The flash goes off. The camera catches Kouri mid-laugh. I attach Kouri's mug shot to his ID card and he goes on his merry way to get it laminated.

I catch a whiff of Calvin Klein's Obsession for Men. Of all the colognes I've sampled, it's the only one I'd buy if I could afford it. The man with the cologne looks like he just finished playing football with the Kennedys in Hyannis. His white polo top is fluorescent against his Coppertone tan. His khaki shorts stop mid-gam like he's been on safari. His golden brown hair looks wind-swept even though there hasn't been a breeze in a week. I wouldn't be surprised if he's an *International Male* catalogue model.

"Boys," he says with a smile that could light Vegas. His blues eyes hone in on Tom. "And who might you be?"

Tom's mouth hangs open. Whatever questions Tom had about which way his rainbow flag flies have been answered.

"That's Tom," I say. "And I'm Dwayne."

Mr. International Male doesn't see me. I'm just the help. Of all the attractive men who have walked through here today, this guy is the first to throw Tom off his game. I'd hoped to endear myself to Tom more before something like this happened. Calvin Klein over here clearly has other ideas.

"I'm Kent. Kent Eastmoore," he says to Tom like he's James Bond.

"Can't eat more?" I say.

"Kent East-moore," he annunciates like I don't speak English.

"Oh. The way you said it, it sounded like 'can't eat more,'" I say. It's the most attitude I've flung all day. "Smile for the camera."

Tom takes his picture. Kent's eyes linger on Tom's as he waits for me to attach the photo to his badge. When I'm done, I wave the card in front of Kent's face to break the spell.

"See you around," Kent says to Tom, smiling like a man who's never wanted for anything. I feel so invisible right now.

"You were kind of mean to him, don't you think?" Tom says after Kent leaves.

"Guys like that bring it out of me," I say. "He reminds me of those good-looking douchebags from *Risky Business*. They never get what they deserve."

"I liked *Risky Business*," Tom says.

Tom looks like he's seeing the real me. I'm worried he doesn't like it. This is exactly what I was afraid would happen. We've had such a fun day volunteering. I'd hate for it to be ruined over something as stupid as a Tom Cruise movie or some smooth operator from the States. I hate this about myself, but I'm not jealous just because Tom is interested in someone other than me. It's that there's a line of men waiting for him to give them the time of day. I've never had that. I probably never will.

"My uncle is having a dinner party later if you want to come," Tom says.

"Will he mind?"

"He made a point of telling me to invite you. I forgot with all the excitement from the day."

Did Tom really forget to invite me or was he just waiting to see if he wanted to spend more time with me? At this point I don't care. Mom's working till midnight. Dinner is dinner.

"I'd love to," I tell him.

Thurlow Street

"Gina!"

I look for Raven on the crowded sidewalk. Athletes have only begun arriving for the Games, and the West End already feels like Manhattan.

"Did you see there's a line to get into Little Sisters?" Raven says when she catches up to me. "Can you believe that?"

"Dwayne said Team Australia charted two planes and Team Germany chartered one," I tell her. "What happened to Fred? I haven't seen him since we got our ID badges."

"He went home to make dinner for us," Raven says. "We better get in that line at Little Sisters before they sell out of tickets for everything."

"Told you we should have come sooner," I say.

"Yeah, whatever."

We walk a quarter of a block to the old house on Thurlow where Little Sisters is located. The rickety stairs to the store were intended for a Victorian family and their servants, not thousands of gay athletes in micro-shorts and tank tops. The people coming back down the stairs have to suck in their guts and flatten themselves against the wall to get past the line to get in.

Betty Baxter is coming down the stairs, her back against the opposite wall. Betty sits on the board of directors for the Gay Games. She got fired from coaching the Canadian Women's Olympic volleyball team for being gay. Raven got to know Betty as part of a team of lesbians who wanted to make sure the Games were accessible to people from all different incomes and walks of life.

"How are you holding up?" Raven asks Betty on her way down.

"We met with CSIS this morning to go over any potential terrorist threats," Betty says.

"Any cause for concern?" Raven asks.

"Nothing serious. They told us to have a good Games."

Betty waves to Raven as she is sucked back outside through the entrance to the stairwell.

"Seems like it was only yesterday we had secret women's parties with passwords to get in," Raven says. "Now look at us, waiting in line for tickets to go line dancing at The Lotus."

On a normal day, Little Sisters is where you come to find listings for roommates, health brochures, and copies of *Angles,* the gay rag. The line going into the store snakes around the bookshelves, making browsing nearly impossible. I'm glad the store is making some coin off the Games. Canada Customs has been seizing gay books at the border; it's left plenty of room on the shelves. Raven told me the store is surviving on sales of cigarettes, sex toys, and poppers.

Raven and I join the line for the cash register next to

a display case full of dildos. We're trying to get tickets for the Women's Culture concert at the Orpheum. I'm hoping there's still tickets to see Alison Bechdel talk about "Dykes to Watch Out For."

"I'm thinking about getting my own place," I tell Raven.

"Stop the presses!" Raven says. "Gina is actually making sense for a change."

"Don't gloat."

"Why the change of heart?"

"I'm afraid either my mom or I is going to say something we can never take back," I say. "Mom drives me up the wall. But I love her."

"And how will she handle you living on your own?"

"She'll hate it more than having a lesbian daughter."

"You're eighteen. There's nothing she can do to stop you."

"I don't know if I'm ready," I tell her. "Living at home has its advantages. I can afford clothes I like. I can save money for school. I don't even know if I can afford rent with what I make at the deli."

"So you get a second job and you take out a student loan," Raven says. "You want us to stop calling you Baby Girl, then start acting like an adult."

I notice a pair of eyes over the top of the book shelf. She's blonde. Femme but she could coach field hockey. She's pretty, which isn't how I would describe most of the women I'm attracted to. And she's older. Probably in her early twenties. I don't think of myself as attractive. When someone shows interest in me, I always question it.

"I love your bandana," the blonde says. "It makes you look like Rosie the Riveter."

"That's where I got the idea from!" I say. "You're the first person to notice."

"You from around here?" the blonde asks.

"How can you tell?" I ask.

"You have a mellow vibe about you," she says. Her friend rolls her eyes and pulls the bill of her cap over her brow, embarrassed. "The people here seem very chill."

"Have you seen us drive?" Raven says. "That'll change your opinion of us."

"Mind your own business," I tell Raven. "Where are you from?"

"Boston, Massachusetts," says the blonde.

"You don't sound like they do on *Cheers*," I say, regretting it as soon as it comes out of my mouth.

"Did you learn everything you know about America from sitcoms?" she teases. I'm a little offended, but definitely interested.

"No, *Schoolhouse Rock!*" Raven says.

The line lurches forward. Instead of being across from the blonde, I am now behind her. She leans her face out from the line. Looking back at me, she says, "Maybe you can show me around Vancouver sometime." And then she faces forward again, returning her attention to the line.

"When did you become such a player?" Raven asks.

"Just now."

"Don't get so popular we can't hang out anymore," Raven says. Like that would ever happen.

Minutes go by without the blonde looking back. I feel the moment has passed. She was probably caught up in the excitement of being around so many gay people at one time. She must have got carried away. I watch her pay for a *Nobody Knows I'm Gay* T-shirt and some tickets. We lock eyes as she leaves the store to go back down the stairs.

A burst of air hits me in the face. It's Raven.

"Timbre's here," she says.

"What? Where?" I panic, looking around like I can't find my child.

"Just reminding you about the last time you fell in love at first sight," Raven says. "Cool your panties, Baby Girl. Opening ceremonies isn't for another twenty-four hours."

Bute Street

Laughter is coming through the screen door when we get to the green house on Bute Street. I can hear Anne Murray playing on the stereo. Tom holds the door open for me. The house smells like basil and garlic. A cork pops. A big hairy shadow is blocking the hallway.

"Oy! I know you two!"

It's Kouri, the Australian wrestler from registration.

"I'm your billet," he says, picking Tom up and squeezing him. "How wild is that, mate? Come on! Everyone's outside."

We follow Kouri down the hall to the back porch. Fred is sitting in a lawn chair. Raven is there, and so is Gina. Gina is smiling at me like she doesn't remember my name. I hate that. The couple of times I've seen her with Raven I got the impression she wasn't interested in me because I'm not a lesbian. She did date the infamous and overrated Timbre, after all. But then I had such a good time with her and Tom on her birthday.

"Dwayne!" Raven says.

"Hey, Raven," I say. "Hey Gina."

"We're going to hang out in the living room if you don't mind," Tom tells his uncle. "We've been taking pictures of people all day and could use some down time."

I follow Tom back into the house even though it's cooler outside. I wonder if I should invite Gina to join us. Tom goes into the kitchen and grabs some bottles of fizzy water. He looks around and then grabs a Kokanee from the fridge. He swiftly cracks open the bottle and divides it between two glasses with the precision of a NASA scientist. We sneak our beers into the living room. Tom clinks his beer glass against mine and then he takes a seat in a big leather armchair.

We're exhausted, but a good exhausted. Like how I

feel after we close A&B Sound on Boxing Day. Between the heat and the beer I already have a buzz. Gina comes into the living room holding three bottles of beer.

"Mind if I join?" Gina asks.

"Make yourself at home," I say, scooching over on the couch.

She hands us each a beer and sits next to me, legs spread apart like she's one of the guys. I never noticed this before, but Gina really knows how to rock a bandana.

"So why did you run away from home, Tom?" Gina asks, taking a swig from her beer.

"You cut right to the chase, don't you?" I say.

"Enquiring minds want to know," she says.

Tom lifts the bottom of his shirt to let in the breeze from the fan. I try not to look, but my eyes are drawn to the smooth six-pack that is his stomach. He holds the cold beer to his forehead before taking a sip.

"I was at a pool party," Tom says. "And my friend Aiden stripped down to his underwear and jumped in the pool. When he came back out, I got a hard-on and everyone could see it in my wet shorts. And then my buddy, Scott, shouts, 'Hey everybody, Tommy has a hard-on for Aiden.'"

"We have a few Scotts at my school," I say.

"It was like every lie I ever told myself was exposed. I tried laughing it off, but anyone with eyes could tell I was panicking inside. I don't even like Scott. The only reason I hang out with him is because of Aiden."

"Do you have a boy crush on Aiden?" Gina asks. She's teasing Tom, but like a sister, not a bully.

"No," he says, too quickly at first. "Maybe just a little."

"A guy in my grade told everyone I gave him a blowjob at a party," I say. "Which was impossible because I wasn't invited to that party. That's when I stopped pretending I was straight."

"The guys at my school used to call me Va-Gina," says Gina. "And the girls used to do this to me in the change room." Gina holds up two fingers in the peace sign and sticks her tongue through it.

"Did they really?" Tom asks.

"Yup."

"That's nasty," Tom says, laughing.

"I couldn't wait to graduate from that hell hole," Gina says.

"Screw those assholes," I say.

"I'll drink to that," says Tom.

We clink the necks of our bottles together.

"Have you two heard of a band called Deee-Lite?" I say. "Album comes out this week."

"I think I saw the video for their song on MuchMusic," Gina says.

"I have the cassette in my bag," I say. "Do you mind if I put it on?"

"Go for it!" says Tom.

I fast-forward the tape to "Groove Is in the Heart"

and start dancing to it. Gina gets up and starts dancing with me. She holds out her hand for Tom to join us, but he waves us away. Gina and I grab a hand each and pull Tom up to his feet. Tom moves to the music, looking self-conscious. He's cute when he's insecure. When the song is over, I rewind the tape and we dance to it again. Tom and Gina sing along to the chorus this time around.

We fall back onto the couch when the song is over.

"We should go to Celebrities," Gina says.

"What's Celebrities?" Tom asks.

"It's a dance club at Davie and Burrard," I tell him. I ask Gina, "Do you think we'll be able to get in?"

"Only one way to find," she says.

"Want to go to a gay bar, Tom?" I ask him.

He looks at us, concerned. He so obviously wants to go, but Mississauga, his dad, and the memory of his hard-on at the pool party are holding him back.

"Didn't you run away to embrace this?" Gina says.

"I'll see if Gaetan can get us into the bar," Tom says. "Promise me you won't say anything to my uncle during dinner. I'll tell him when I come home."

"Like how you called your parents to tell them why you took off?" I remind Tom.

"I knew I shouldn't have told you that," he says. "Not a word about that either."

"What did I miss?" Gina asks.

"Hey kids, dinner is ready," Fred says, scaring the

hell out of us. "The three of you look like you've seen a ghost."

"We were just talking about what we wanted to play next on the stereo," Tom says.

"What's wrong with this music?" Fred says about Deee-Lite. "It's got a beat and you can dance to it. Now come along, kids. Dinner is getting cold."

Saturday August 4, 1990
Opening Ceremonies

Bikini Beach

I wake up to the sound of the ocean licking the shore. There's sand in my socks and underwear. My arm is asleep. I look down to see Dwayne, his head tucked under my shoulder, his head against my chest. Gina is curled up against the log I'm leaning against. It feels like the end of *Planet of the Apes*.

"Where are we?" I ask.

Gina and Dwayne poke their heads up like chickens. Dwayne yawns and says, "Bikini Beach. It's coming back to me now. I wanted to cool my feet in the ocean."

"I need to get home!" Gina says, brushing the sand off her. "My parents are going to kill me."

"Mom is probably waiting to dial the last number in

nine-one-one," Dwayne says. "I have to work until two and then I'm volunteering for Opening Ceremonies tonight. What about you guys?"

"I'm entering the stadium with Raven and Fred," Gina says.

"I haven't thought that far ahead," I say.

"I'm sure there's going to be a party at your uncle's house after," Gina says. "Why don't we all meet there after Opening Ceremonies?"

"Sounds like a plan," I say.

"I love how you both just included me in your plans," Dwayne says. "I feel like I'm in a gang."

The three of us hurry back to our different parts of town. I take off my shoes and tip-toe up the porch steps of my uncle's house, but the steps squeak like a rusty wheel. The front door is just as loud. It doesn't matter. Uncle Fred is already awake. I can smell the coffee from the front door. I try creeping up the stairs just the same.

"Did you really think I didn't notice you were out all night?" Uncle Fred shouts from the kitchen. "Get in here!"

Uncle Fred and Kouri are seated at the kitchen table. Kouri is already showered and dressed in another jumper. Today's pattern is pink flamingos.

"Where were you last night?" Uncle Fred demands.

"Celebrities," I tell him. "Gina invited me and Dwayne."

"Gaetan already told me he got you three into the bar," Fred says. "Where did you come from just now?"

"We fell asleep on the beach."

"Aww. That's sort of cute, no?" Kouri says to Uncle Fred, buttering him up.

"It's adorable, but what if your parents called?" Uncle Fred asks. "What was I supposed to tell them?"

"Sorry. We were having such a good time. I danced on a speaker! I didn't mean to stay out all night."

"Tom, you have to promise me you're not going to die on this trip," Uncle Fred says. "Your father is already suspicious of me. Even though I don't visit home as much as I should, the door is still open. If you die, your father and grandparents will never speak to me again."

"You're overreacting," I say. "I sneak into bars all the time at home."

"Home is your parents' jurisdiction," Uncle Fred says. "This house is mine. Promise me you're not going to die while you're under this roof."

"I promise," I say.

"And maybe go easy on the Daisy Dukes," Uncle Fred says. "There's more chicken hawks in town than usual."

"What's that supposed to mean?" I ask.

"It means you're dressed like jail bait," Kouri says in his friendly growl without looking up from the Gay Games issue of *Angles*.

"What's on the gay agenda for today?" Uncle Fred asks Kouri.

"There's a leathermen's brunch at the Heritage House

and a cocktail party at the Royal, and of course the Opening Ceremonies."

"That reminds me," I say. "I don't know what I'm doing tonight. Everyone I know is either in the Opening Ceremonies or volunteering at them."

"What do you want to do, Tommy?" Uncle Fred asks.

"I feel like I'm expected to volunteer at the Opening Ceremonies," I say. "But I actually really want to go to the ceremonies as a spectator."

"Then go get a ticket at Little Sisters and go with Gaetan," Fred says.

"How much is a ticket? Like, fifty dollars?"

"They're ten. It's the Gay Games, not the Vancouver Canucks," Fred says.

"Why does the gay paper here spell women as *wimin*, with two Is instead of an O and an A?" Kouri asks.

"It's a Vancouver thing," Fred says. "We're very live-and-let-live here."

"Sign me up for some of that," Kouri says.

Fourth Avenue

I tell the cab driver to let me out on the block behind our house. I check to make sure no one is looking, and then I dash past the house behind ours and hop the fence into our backyard. I stay low as I make my way toward my bedroom window. The window is still unlocked like I left it yesterday.

The curtain whooshes to the side. My heart stops in anticipation of seeing my mother's face. It's my sister, Marcella. I climb through the window into my room.

"Have you lost your mind staying out all night?" she whispers. "Mom already doesn't trust you."

"Is she awake?"

"Not yet, thank the Lord. What's wrong with you? It's like you're *trying* to piss her off."

"I could say the same thing about her." I flop onto my bed and push my face into my pillow. "Now get out of my room. I need my beauty sleep for Opening Ceremonies."

"I'm worried about you," Marcella says. "This is the third night in a row you've been out partying."

"I'm being my true self. You're just not used to it."

"I'm trying to keep the peace. I get that this isn't the coolest place in town, but it's a roof over your head. Your friends can't give you that."

Raven would. Fred probably would too.

"What would you say if I moved out of the house," I ask my sister.

"Before marriage?"

I roll my eyes at Marcella. She hits her forehead with the heel of her hand, realizing her blunder.

"I'd still say you're nuts," she says. "You have so much going for you. You're smart. You're athletic. You're pretty."

"I'm not pretty."

"Yes, you are! Maybe not in the traditional sense, but you're an attractive woman. It doesn't take a lesbian to see that. Don't throw away what you have so you can party."

"It's not about partying," I say. "It's about living my life how I want to."

"You've made it eighteen years here. You can last a couple more until you have money for university."

"Easy for you to say. You're mom's favourite. I don't know if I'll make it here till I'm twenty."

Marcella lies down on the bed and puts her arm around my waist. We used to watch scary movies like this when we were kids.

"I will never know what it's like to walk in your shoes," Marcella says. "And if you were straight, I'd say go for it. But if you move out of this house right now, Mom might never let you back in."

That's what's been holding me back. My mom could never live with herself if she kicked me out of the house, even if I was the worst person on Earth. If I leave, I'll be doing my parents a favour. When I go, I want to make sure it's on my own terms.

Seymour Street

Thank God I slept on the beach, or I don't know how I'd make it through my shift at A&B Sound. I managed to sneak in a few more z's after Mom finished yelling at me for staying out all night. I thought she'd have been happy for me since I was making friends.

"Dwayne!" Justice says as he unlocks the door to let me into the store.

"What? I'm early."

"I was going to say I'm surprised to see you here," he says. "You might want to blend your concealer more. You're painted like Tammy Faye Bakker."

"*Merde!* That obvious?" I say, rushing up the stairs toward the staff bathroom. "I was trying to hide the bags under my eyes."

"Did you go dancing?" Justice asks, two steps behind me.

"A bartender at Celebrities gave me a VIP card so I can get in without ID," I gloat. "Me and my new friends, Tom and Gina, have gone dancing three nights in a row."

"You are so obviously in love with that guy Tom," he says. Justice can barely contain his jealousy.

"Am not!" I say, dabbing at the makeup under my eyes to soften it.

"My lady doth protest too much."

"It's *milady*! If you're going to quote Shakespeare, the least you could do is not sound like a hillbilly."

"I thought you liked hillbillies since you like Daisy Dukes. Isn't that what you told me your new boyfriend wears all the time?"

"Stop it!" I walk past Justice and put my name tag on. "We're just friends."

"That's what you said about Warren and the moment he got a girlfriend you did everything in your power to break them up. And where's Warren now?"

"Is it even legal for you to be talking about my personal life like this?"

"We talk about guys all the time."

"Tom is different. I admit that I went a little crazy with Warren, but I learned my lesson. Tom isn't even sure if he's gay."

"He flew all the way across Canada at the last minute for the Gay Games. It's safe to say he's gay."

"Why must you torture me so?"

"I'm trying to protect you. It was hard watching you get rejected by Warren. Do you know how many of your mistakes I've covered for you? People were complaining!"

"I didn't know that. Thank you."

"It's fine. Even on your worst day you work harder than most people on their best. But you need to stop chasing the unattainables. Guys who look like us …"

"As in ugly?"

"As in unconventionally attractive," he says. "Our best bet is to stick to our own."

"You mean settle."

"Call it whatever you want, but don't complain about how good attractive people have it, and then chase them around like a lap dog." Justice looks at his watch. "We open in ten minutes. If you're planning on having a crappy cup of coffee from the break room I suggest you do it now."

I curse Justice under my breath as he walks away. I don't know if I'm mad at him because he implied I'm ugly or because he told me to settle. But the fact that he had the guts to say what he said is the most attractive he's been to me since I started working here.

Bute Street

Uncle Fred, Kouri, Gaetan, and I are standing on the front porch looking up at the sky. It's the cloudiest it's been since I arrived in Vancouver. Uncle Fred is not amused.

"I really hope the weather doesn't give those holy rollers the satisfaction of raining on our Opening Ceremonies," he says.

"The stadium is covered, ain't it?" Kouri says.

"That's not the point," Fred says. "I want to believe their God is on our side."

"You see a UFO?" Raven asks, standing on the sidewalk in front of the gate. She's dressed in the Team Vancouver uniform — puffy white pants and a sweatshirt with the Gay Games logo on it.

"You look like you're going parachuting," Gaetan says.

"No," Kouri adds. "She looks like her husband left her after twenty-five years."

"I've never seen you look so feminine," says Uncle Fred.

"This is what I get for being a team player," Raven says. "What about you, Tom? Want to get a dig in too?"

"Both of you and my uncle look like you're in a cult," I say.

"Atta boy," Gaetan says, slapping my shoulder. "Look at you throwing shade!"

"I thought the uniform brought out the colour of my eyes," Uncle Fred says.

"Thanks for the compliments, guys," Raven says sarcastically.

"Oh, relax," Fred says. "We're just yanking your chain because we know you'd never be caught dead in this outfit were it not for the Games."

"Where's Gina?" I ask.

"She's meeting us at the stadium," Raven says. She opens the front gate for us. "All aboard, boys. Next stop: BC Place Stadium."

The sidewalks are bustling. They've only been getting busier since Wednesday. A multitude of coloured uniforms walk by. Reds, greens, and golds. They remind me of unitards from cheesy seventies sci-fi movies. Vancouver does feel like a city of the future. Different races are mingling. Same-sex couples are holding hands. Everyone is … happy. This is it how it must feel to be completely straight. To not have a secret. To not have to pretend.

My heart beats faster as we get closer to the stadium. It's as though we're being pulled toward it like a magnet. People are carrying flags from around the world. They blow horns and whistles. They break into dance. I'm getting emotional. I'm happy, but I can feel tears stinging the corners of my eyes. I'm so glad Dad's not here to see this.

"We need to find the athlete's entrance," Fred says when we arrive at the stadium. "This is where we part ways."

"I'll meet you guys back at the house," I say.

"Please don't let my nephew get abducted by a herd of horny Australians," Uncle Fred says.

"Oy! Why do they have to be Australian?" Kouri protests.

I watch as Uncle Fred, Raven, and Kouri walk off in their uniforms. They are the least likely athletes I'd expect to see at an international sports competition. It makes me all the more happy for them.

BC Place Stadium

I remember sitting on the couch with my mom watching the BC Place Opening Ceremonies on TV. It was this endless parade of dancers and singers, vintage cars, and marching bands. We got our first glimpse of Expo Ernie, the official mascot of Expo '86. I was ten and nearly peed my pants when I saw the life-sized robot.

"How are those ladies skating?" I asked Mom, still wearing her nurse's uniform from St. Paul's.

"It's artificial ice, Dwayne," Mom yawned, her eyes barely open. "They used to skate on it all the time on *Donny & Marie*."

Even at ten, I knew the stadium wasn't built for people like me. BC Place was for football and soccer games; home shows and rock concerts; and for the straight people who went to those sorts of things. Had you told me that one day be I'd be escorting seven thousand gay athletes into that very stadium, I would have laughed in your face.

My job is to help regulate the number of athletes entering the stadium at one time. The stadium's white, quilted dome is supported by fans. I'm one of the volunteers responsible for making sure the air pressure inside the stadium never changes so the dome doesn't collapse. To do this, we have to escort athletes in groups through the stadium's basement where they board a freight elevator big enough to hold a yacht. From there, the athletes are whisked to the ground level of the stadium where they will make their entrance.

I'm coming back from having dropped a group of athletes at the freight elevator. Even with thousands of athletes and spectators, the Christian protestors are out shaking their fists and posters at us. The lady with the sandwich board is with them. Poor thing. She needs a gay best friend. I've stopped feeling threatened by them. Instead I feel sorry for them.

"Dwayne!" Gina is hopping up and down. The Team Vancouver uniform is doing nothing for her figure. She doesn't need to know that, though.

"I think you're my last group," I say, hugging Gina, Raven, and Fred. "How long have you been waiting to get in?"

"Over an hour," Raven says. "My knees are killing me."

"You're almost there, girl," I say. "Mary said that k.d. lang has a box."

"Get out!" Gina says.

"Said she saw her with her own eyes."

"Are you seriously telling me I'm going to be in the same stadium with k.d. lang?" Gina asks, hyperventilating.

"She would never risk ruining her career by coming to the Gay Games," Raven says, skeptically. "She got rid of the pink streak in her hair to go on the Tommy Hunter show."

Another volunteer signals to me that I can lead the group into the stadium.

"Look in the sky," Fred shouts, pointing upwards.

I'm afraid to look up. What if it's the ball of fire Pastor Birch predicted in his newspaper ad? I look skyward. It is the exact opposite. The sun is starting to peek through the clouds. And there's not one, but two, rainbows.

BC Place Stadium

"Some guy in the bathroom said k.d. lang has a box," Gaetan says, taking his seat in time to do the wave for the millionth time.

"Who's k.d. lang?" I ask.

"Tom!" Gaetan says, outraged. "k.d. lang is not only the greatest singer since Patsy Cline, she's Canadian ... and a lesbian."

"Never heard of her."

"*Les enfants de nos jours*," Gaetan says.

The athletes have been entering the stadium for close to an hour. It is a parade of formations; flags, hats, bright-coloured clothes, and umbrellas. Instead of entering by country, the athletes enter by city. Indiana is followed by Barcelona, which is followed by Bombay. Watching the athletes wave up to us gives me the same tingling feeling of pride I felt when I heard "Go West" on the cassette player in my car a week ago. I feel like I'm a part of something bigger than me. Like we're changing the world.

"How are the swimming practices with your uncle?" Gaetan asks. "Can he win a medal?"

"I doubt it," I say. "I've never met an athlete who didn't care about winning."

"He only registered because he tested positive," Gaetan says.

"Positive for what?" I ask. "Does Uncle Fred have AIDS?"

"*Non, non, non…*" Gaetan says. "This is not my place to say."

"Please," I say. "I won't tell him you told me."

Gaetan looks into my eyes like he's debating what to say.

"I'm only telling you because you are part of the family," he says. "I would never disclose another person's status. But your uncle has HIV, not AIDS. We both do. And Fred does care about the competition, but for different reasons than winning. He is proving to himself the virus will not defeat him. So are many of the men who are competing. They didn't come here just to win a medal. They came here to change the face of AIDS."

I don't care which place I finish, I can hear Uncle Fred saying to me at the pool. *As long as I finish strong.*

I see the Games in a new light now. On television, we've been force-fed images of people dying of AIDS. Skeletons in hospital beds, like Holocaust victims, attached to tubes. A warning to those of us who aren't out yet, those of us who are still questioning what we are. And yet here I am in a stadium with seven thousand rosy-cheeked athletes. Some of them, like my uncle, determined to finish strong, no matter what place they come in.

There is a break in the parade of athletes.

"And now, ladies and gentlemen," the MC says over the loudspeakers. "TEAM VANCOUVER!"

The stadium erupts into one giant cheer. We are on

our feet shouting at the top of our lungs. I can barely see the stadium floor for all the hand and flag waving. I look at Gaetan. Tears are streaming down his cheeks.

I press the palm of my hand against his face and show him his tears. He presses his hand against mine and holds it up for me to see. It's wet with my own tears. After holding down my emotions all these years, it feels good to finally cry. Gaetan drapes his arm over my shoulder like it's the last day of school. I've never enjoyed being intimate with another guy before. We keep cheering, searching for Fred, Gina, and Raven as they enter the stadium.

BC Place Stadium

I've played softball since Grade Nine. I've been in tournaments before, but this is insane. Dwayne escorts us into a giant cement tunnel toward to a giant freight elevator.

"Keep walking to the other side of the elevator," Dwayne tells the athletes ahead of us.

My fingers go numb and I feel light-headed, like the first sip of beer I snuck from a bottle when my parents weren't looking. I try not to pant. What if the Gay Games are some right-wing Christian plot and the elevator is really taking us to a concentration camp? As I cross the threshold of the elevator, I feel like I'm stepping into the unknown. I look back at Dwayne, who is smiling from ear to ear. Dwayne would never sell us out to the Christians.

"That uniform does wonders for you figure," he shouts over the athletes entering the elevator.

It's funny because he's lying.

The elevator doors close. Raven takes my hand and Fred's and squeezes them tight. There's a jolt and we start our climb. It feels like the last minutes before midnight on New Year's Eve. There are nervous giggles in the elevator. We can already hear the crowd. I stare at the doors, waiting for them to open. Another jolt and we come to a halt. The doors part. A cheer goes up.

We follow Team Victoria down a tunnel toward the stadium floor. I can see the light from the entrance at the end of the tunnel. Team Calgary, dressed in lime green cowboy shirts and white cowboy hats, is making their way around the stadium. Farther ahead are clusters of pink track suits and bright blue jackets. The cheers of the crowd get louder as we get closer and closer to the end of the tunnel.

"This is what it must feel like to exit the birth canal," Fred says.

We are the last team to enter the stadium. A volunteer tells us to wait a moment before we enter. Team Victoria makes its entrance, and then after a couple of minutes, Team Vancouver is allowed to enter the stadium.

It's like we're entering the Colosseum in Roman times. Flashbulbs flicker like stars. Flags flutter. Frisbees are thrown. A beach ball bounces off the fingertips of the athletes, making its way around the stadium. I feel like royalty for playing shortstop in fast pitch. I've dreamed of competing in the Olympics. But I never dreamed I would get to experience anything like this.

This feeling of love and adoration is how it must feel for Timbre when she's on stage. I shake the image of her face from my memory. This is my moment. I refuse to let her move in on it.

We do a lap around the stadium and join the other athletes on the AstroTurf. Scrims painted with the Vancouver skyline serve as a backdrop for the stage. Hot air balloons with *Celebration '90* float above the cartoon skyline. On the right side of the stage is a white staircase leading up to a cauldron.

I shield my eyes from the stadium lights to see if I can find k.d. lang in the box seats. I can see what I think is a big-boned girl from Alberta, but it's hard to tell.

"Stop looking for k.d. lang," Raven says.

There are choirs and line dancers and square dancers and Native dancers. Every gay choir, chorus, band, and dance troupe has come here to perform on the world stage. "Memory" from *Cats* plays over video tributes to Dr. Tom Waddell, the founder of the Gay Games. A white horse is paraded through the stadium in honour of those we lost to AIDS. In the time it takes for Carole Pope to sing a song, we are reminded this isn't just a competition, it's a fight for our lives.

An even larger choir takes the stage to sing "When Tomorrow Comes" from *Les Misérables*. Mom loves that album and plays it all the time at home and in the car. Hearing it now, performed by queer singers from all over the world, brings a lump to my throat.

The song ends. Two runners enter the stadium carrying the torch, which is relayed to another pair of runners, who carry it up to the cauldron. It's not going to light! I panic. The Games are ruined! But the fire catches and the cauldron erupts into a flame.

And now to get all seven thousand of us out of the stadium. I look up once more to the boxes to see if I can find k.d. lang. A figure looks down at us. I swear its k.d.'s haircut.

"Well, if it isn't Rosie the Riveter!"

I look over and see the blonde from Little Sisters. Raven and Fred are lost in the crowd.

"I don't feel like Rosie in this outfit," I say.

"Your ass definitely looks better in denim," she says, blushing. "I don't know what's gotten into me. I'm way more conservative at home. It must be the fresh Canadian air."

"I'm Gina."

"Georgia." She sticks out her hand in this awkward and adorable way. I shake it. Her palms are cool despite the heat.

"What did you think of the ceremonies?" I ask.

"I kind of feel like Mariel Hemingway in *Personal Best*," she says.

"Totally," I say. "What sport are you competing in?"

"Fast-pitch," Georgia says. "I'm the pitcher for the Boston Flamingos."

There's like forty-two sports being played over the next eight days. Of course she's playing fast pitch.

"I play shortstop for Team S.O.S., Vancouver," I say.

"I should have known," she says. "I have a thing for shortstops."

"Georgia! C'mon," a Boston accent shouts over the crowd. "Let's get to the bars!"

"I'll see you on the field," Georgia says. She winks at me and wiggles her fingers goodbye. The crowd envelops her, and she is gone.

Back outside, the warm summer air feels good on my skin. The city lights are twinkling. The stadium parking lot is aflutter with giggles and cheers and dancing. A small cluster of drunk people are singing "We Are the Champions." Slowly, the crowd begins fanning out in the direction of the gay and lesbian bars. I've never felt so safe being out on the street in all my life.

Sunday
August 5, 1990

Bute Street

"Oy!" Kouri says as I enter the kitchen. He's been with us three days and already claimed a space next to Uncle Fred at the kitchen table. Today's shirt, shorts, and socks pattern is Marilyn Monroe.

"What's on the gay agenda today, Kouri?" Uncle Fred asks without looking up from *The Vancouver Sun*.

"Today is killah," he growls. "There's a WESA T-dance at the West End community centre. What's a WESA?"

"West End Softball Association," Uncle Fred says.

"I might go to that," he says. "And this evening there's the Mr. and Mrs. Vancouver Leather contest at Graceland. I have tickets for "Floating with The Buoys," the men's chorus cruise, because I like a nice choir. And Jane Rule, David Watmough, and Alan Hollinghurst will be at the opening of Words Without Borders. I quite liked *The Swimming-Pool Library*."

"*The Young in One Another's Arms* by Jane Rule is the best book set in Vancouver," Uncle Fred says. "And Jane was very vocal about making sure alternative voices were represented at the Games."

"Oh and look!" Kouri says. "Today is the first day of the swimming competition!"

"Don't remind me," Fred says.

"Boys in Speedos," Gaetan says, coming into the kitchen in just his Jockeys. "You should go, Tom. It will be the hottest spot in town."

"I was thinking of going," I say. "I am a swimmer."

"I thought you played water polo," Kouri says.

"That involves swimming," I tell him.

"You don't have to make excuses to see beautiful men," Gaetan says, pouring himself a cup of coffee.

"Gaetan ... live and let live," says Uncle Fred.

"Actually, Gaetan's right," I say. "I do want to see boys in Speedos."

Gaetan raises his coffee cup in my direction and winks at me.

We are all startled when the yellow rotary wall phone rings. In one fluid motion, Uncle Fred leans back in his chair, raises his left arm over his shoulder like he's doing the back stroke, and grabs the receiver without even looking. The chair's front legs clunk onto the floor back to a seated position, the receiver clutched between Fred's ear and shoulder.

"Señor Schneider is no in casa," he says, laughing at his own bad Spanish accent. "Oh, hey Fraser. How's it goin'? … I have a car but I don't have time to drive to Burnaby. I promised Raven I'd volunteer at the Queer Arts Festival today."

"I'll do it!" I say.

"Do what?" Uncle Fred asks.

"Drive someone," I say. "I don't mind."

"Can I call you back in five minutes, Fraser?" Uncle Fred hangs up the phone and says to me, "Before you say yes I just want to make sure you know you'll be driving to Burnaby. You'll be getting on the highway."

"I drive on the 401 all the time."

"Believe it or not I own a pickup," Uncle Fred says.

"I don't believe it," Kouri says.

"A client gave me the title in lieu of payment," Uncle Fred explains. There's something you should know about Bill..."

"Just tell me who I'm picking up, where I'm picking him up, where I'm taking him, and how to get there," I say, interrupting my uncle the way my dad interrupts me when he wants me to stop talking.

"Fine then," Uncle Fred says, closing the paper.

"You'll be picking Bill Monroe up at his apartment at Nelson and Bidwell and driving him to the Riverway Sports Park for the Opening Ceremonies of the softball tournament."

"Another Opening Ceremonies?"

"It's a gay sports tournament. What do you expect?" Kouri says.

"I'll call Fraser and let him know you'll do it," Fred says. "And you're going to love the El Camino. It looks like something Daisy Duke would drive on *The Dukes of Hazzard*."

Third Avenue

I'm wearing my team cap, shorts, and socks. My jersey is in my equipment bag with my glove and bat. I check myself out in the bathroom mirror before breakfast. I look more butch than usual for around the house, but I'm tired of changing identities every time I walk out the door.

Mom is already awake and dressed for church. I can hear dad snoring. The kitchen smells of fried eggs, bacon, and toast. Mom looks at me as I enter the kitchen.

"You look like a boy," she says.

"I look like a softball player," I tell her.

"You'll never find a man dressed like that," she says.

"Mom … I haven't even had a cup of coffee yet."

"It wouldn't kill you to look like a woman," she says.

"I do look like a woman," I say. "What I don't look like is a wife."

That was probably a little harsh for first thing in the morning. I wish she knew how hard I'm trying to get along. She's my mother and I love her. Whatever we're going through now doesn't erase all the good memories I have of her. But sometimes I wonder if Mom isn't making it miserable to live here so I'll leave on my own. If that's what she's doing, it's working. But if I do move out, I couldn't afford things like taking a week off from the deli counter to participate in the Games.

"Screw it," I say. "I'll grab a coffee on The Drive. Wish me luck."

"What for?" Mom says, through a mouthful of food.

It's not till I get to the sidewalk I remember Raven is picking me up. I'd go hide from Mom at Josephine's Café, but Raven won't know I'm there. I drop my equipment bag and sit on the curb, feeling like Charlie Brown. The garage door creaks open and Mom pulls out of the driveway in the Chrysler. She looks straight ahead as she backs out onto the street and drives off in the direction of the church.

Canada Way

It's been nothing but rolling hills, cows, farmhouses, and the smell of manure for a mile now.

"Will you please say something?" Bill says. "It's like

driving with Harpo Marx. What did you say your name is again?"

"Tom," I say. "My uncle didn't tell me you were going to be dressed as Queen Elizabeth."

"It's an Opening Ceremony," he says. "Who did you expect? Joan Crawford?"

"When he told me your name is Bill Monroe, I just assumed you'd be dressed like a man."

Bill's painted eyebrow rises into a point, nearly knocking off his blue pillbox hat. He touches the pearls around his neck.

"Well, your first mistake was you volunteered," Bill says.

Bill waves at his face with a silk fan that has the wingspan of an eagle. I'm impressed by the amount of cool air he's able to generate with barely a flick of his wrist. I'm sweating my balls off in a tank top and denim shorts. I can't imagine how hot it must be in his rigid blue dress and stockings.

"Are you okay?" I ask him. "I'm sorry it's so hot in here. The AC doesn't work. I can speed up to cool the cab off if you like."

"I'm windblown enough, thank you," he shouts over the wind. "What sport are you competing in?"

"I'm not competing," I tell him. "I wish I were, though. I love competition."

"I think it's barbaric," Bill says. "I'll stick to dresses and wigs, thank you!"

"Was that you in the convertible at the Opening Ceremonies yesterday?"

"Yes. I was promised a speech but that got cancelled at the last minute," Bill says. "Sabotage, I tell you! They always expect the queens to raise the money and distribute the pamphlets, then tell us take a hike when they hand out the cash."

"If that's how you feel then why do you do it?" I ask.

"Because some things are more important than my ego," Bill says. "And I'm tired of the city sweeping the gays and the dykes under the rug. No more!"

An A&W sign appears on the horizon like a mirage.

"Would you mind if we made a pit stop for something cold to drink?" Bill says.

"You want to go to an A&W dressed like that?"

"What's wrong with the way I'm dressed?"

"It's just that ..."

"Darling, I've been doing this for twenty years. Trust me, no one messes with Queen Elizabeth."

There's no point in arguing. Like it or not, this is what I signed up for. I turn into the driveway of the A&W hoping there's a drive-thru. Instead, it's the old-fashioned kind where you park your car and the servers come to you on roller skates.

"Welcome to A&W," our server says, placing a tray on the window. She sees Bill dressed as the Queen. Her eyes spread open. Her mouth is a perfect O. She stops

94

herself from laughing and plays along. "Welcome, Your Highness. What can I get you today?"

"Could you possibly bring me the largest root beer float you have and whatever my chauffeur would like," Bill says in an English accent that's as crisp as an apple.

"I'll have a root beer float too," I say.

The server is back with our drinks in a matter of minutes. Bill and I sit in the front seat sipping our root beer floats. The brain freeze is exactly what I need. The site of the Queen in the front seat of a pickup turns a few heads, but no one approaches us either, out of fear or respect.

"It's a shame Dr. Waddell didn't live to see the Games being hosted outside of San Francisco," Bill says, holding several napkins under the freezing root beer glass. "He was such a lovely man. He loved Vancouver. He always said it was a beautiful and friendly city."

"Who's he?"

"Dr. Tom Waddell? He started the Gay Games in San Francisco in 1982. He paid a price for it too. The U.S. Olympic Committee sued him for originally calling them the Gay Olympics. They made his life miserable until he died."

"What happened to him?"

"He died of AIDS."

I feel myself grow cold. There's that word again. It's everywhere even when it's not written or spoken. It's there in the red ribbons pinned to shirts, in the initials of organizations that offer support. Even the rainbow flag screams AIDS. I hate it. I wish I had the power to make it stop.

"Now, now," Bill says, sensing my discomfort. "This too shall pass. Trust me on that. I'm assuming you're going to the parade tomorrow."

"Parades aren't my thing."

"You have to go to every Pride whether you like or it not," Bill says. "Otherwise they'll take it away. You have to fight for every single thing we have. Don't ever forget that."

"Okay, I'll go!"

"Enough of that," Bill says. His straw gurgles as it drains the bottom of his glass. "We have a softball tournament to open."

The waitress has cleared our tray and I turn on the ignition.

"I feel like I'm driving Miss Daisy," I say.

"Come closer so I can slap you," Bill says and laughs a big nasal laugh.

Seymour Street

A&B Sound has been open for less than an hour. I'm working the main floor, killing time, running a duster across shelves of *Rhythm Nation 1814*, *The Immaculate Collection*, *Violator* and *I Do Not Want What I Haven't Got*.

Of all my duties at the store, I enjoy this one the most. It's like getting paid to daydream and listen to music.

SNAP!

Justice's thumb and middle fingers vibrate in front of my eyes.

"You look out of it," he says. "You hungover?"

"Just out late again," I say, like my life is one big afterparty.

"Smell you," Justice says. "Did you go to Celebrities again?" he asks. He says "Celebrities" like it's exclusive, instead of the only gay dance club on Davie Street.

"I was at a house party, like it's any of your business."

"Was Tom there?"

"Are we in *Heathers* now?" I ask. "It was his Uncle's house. Gina was there too."

"You're still coming to the Opening Gala of Words Without Borders tonight, right?"

I completely forgot I said yes to that. I should have known better than to commit to anything two weeks before the Games. I only said yes because Justice has a crush on me. It can be annoying, but it's nice to be adored by someone.

"What time is that again?" I ask.

"Eight p.m. at Granville Island Theatre. Don't tell me you forgot. You were the one who said you wanted to go to alternative events instead of the typical buff and shirtless dance parties."

I did say I wanted to go to alternative events. But that was before I started hanging out with Tom and Gina. Now I want to do whatever they want to do.

I catch a whiff of Calvin Klein's Obsession for Men. It can't be. Not this early. Not in this part of town. I look down the aisle and there he is: Kent Eastmoore. The smooth American who would have swallowed Tom whole like a boa constrictor had I not been there.

"Are you listening to me?" Justice says. "I paid ten dollars each for those tickets!"

Kent walks right past me without even noticing. I leave Justice where he is and follow Kent up the stairs where we keep everything that is not top forty. I pretend to dust Loretta Lynn's catalogue and stare at Kent's back while he flips through the dance music. Even his back is beautiful. His shoulder blades look like wings folded across his back. His tapered haircut blends seamlessly into his tanned neck. He could be a model for Bruce Weber. I hate him, but I still want to be him. How screwed is that? I approach him, then I remember the duster in my hand and put it down. The last thing I want is to look like a servant.

"Can I help you find anything?" I ask Kent.

"I'm just browsing for something new and interesting, but I don't think I'm going to find it in this store."

Typical American. Just got to remind the Canadians about how much better the shopping is in the States.

It's not enough that their dollar is worth a dollar thirty Canadian.

"Have you heard of a band named Deee-Lite?" I ask. "I've had *World Clique* on my Walkman for a couple of weeks now."

"I've been listening to them for months," Kent says, waving Deee-Lite away. "I'm friends with a DJ on Fire Island. He's always making me these great mixtapes. I met Lady Miss Kier at a party at David Geffen's."

If it were anyone else telling me this I'd assume they were lying to one-up me. But not Kent. Of course he goes to Fire Island. Of course he knows Lady Miss Kier. Of course he went to a party at David Geffen's. He's probably done coke off the head of an Academy Award.

"You look familiar," he says. "Have we met?"

"Ever been to Fire Island?" I say, trying to be funny.

"Like *you've* been to Fire Island," he says with an arrogant laugh. "Registration! That's it! You were taking pictures with that hot little number."

"Tom. He has a name."

"Thanks for reminding me. I already forgot," Kent says. He starts looking around the store. "Does he work here too?"

"No. He's driving Queen Elizabeth to open the softball tournament, and then he's going to watch some swimming."

"What are you? His secretary?"

"I talked to him on the phone before I went to work," I say.

Of course I didn't tell Tom that Bill Monroe was a drag queen when he told me who he was driving to Burnaby. I thought it would be funnier if he found out for himself.

"Thanks for letting me know where I can find him," Kent says. "I was hoping to run into him again. I was already planning on cheering on my team. We have a back stroker who might break a world record."

Kent walks past me, leaving a trail of cologne. What have I done? I practically handed Tom to him in a bow. I go back down the stairs and nearly run into Justice who is on his way up.

"Where have you been?" he asks.

"Helping a customer," I say. "Hey, do you mind if I meet you at the theatre tonight? There's something I need to take care of after work."

"Does this have anything to do with the Rob Lowe wannabe that just left the store?"

"I need to check on something," I say.

"Whatever. Just remember I was your friend before this Tom guy showed up."

If he's trying to make me feel guilty, it's working. But I still need to get to the Aquatic Centre after work to save Tom from Kent.

Riverway Sports Park

"Thank you, my faithful and loyal subjects," Bill Monroe's English accent echoes across the diamond. He's standing on the pitcher's mound speaking into a microphone wearing a matching blue jacket, skirt, and pillbox hat. A black purse hangs from one forearm. "I was told there would be a lot of queens here, but I appear to be the only one."

Raven elbows me in the ribs and points to Bill. It's Bill's standard opening remarks, but it never ceases to please. Bill is an institution. An appearance by Bill is the gay sports equivalent of singing the national anthem.

The crowd is loving it. Especially the athletes from the Commonwealth countries. I see Georgia on the other side of the diamond with her teammates. She wiggles her fingers hello, like a wallflower at a high school dance. Her ponytail is shiny. Her hair moves like it's in slow motion. It reminds me of the Farrah Fawcett poster hanging on the wall of the barbershop on Commercial. I wiggle my fingers back at her.

"I can take her a note at recess if you like."

Tom is standing over my shoulder, appearing out of nowhere. He's wearing his Daisy Dukes. How does he not know how gay he looks? I want to say something, but I don't want to freak him out. He's been slowly peeking his head out of the closet these last few days. I don't want to risk his pulling it closed even one centimetre.

"Are you here to volunteer?" I say.

"I drove the Queen here," Tom says.

"You drove Bill Monroe here?"

"Yeah. He's really nice. We even made a pitstop at the A&W on the highway."

Tom has a smug look on his face. As if he likes that I'm surprised to learn he was Bill's ride to the park. As if I didn't think he had it in him. Which I didn't.

"What?" Tom says. "Why are you looking at me like that?"

I'm impressed with Tom, but I would never let him know it. Not this soon in our friendship, anyway. I've learned that from hanging out with straight guys. I want to see how cool Tom is with the gay thing when a guy tries to kiss him.

"I didn't know you could drive," I say.

He can tell that I'm bluffing. It's one of the things I like about him.

"Is that the girl from the Opening Ceremonies you were telling me and Dwayne about?" Tom says, looking in Georgia's direction.

"Yeah. So?"

"You know you can't get to third base with her until after the tournament is over, right?" Tom says.

"Thank you!" Raven says.

"Did you invite him here to tell me that?" I ask her.

"I may have let Fraser know Fred had a car and a nephew with a driver's license," Raven says.

"I might be new to this whole gay sports thing," Tom says, "but I've umpired my fair share of girl's softball games. If there's one thing I know, it's that you girls are competitive."

"That's what I've been trying to tell her," Raven says. "Do you really want to throw a hot romance onto that?"

"The tournament doesn't end until Thursday!" I say.

"Didn't you see *Bull Durham*?" Tom says. "Love and baseball don't mix."

"Play ball!" Bill shouts into the microphone.

The crowd begins to disperse. Half the lesbians and their moms head toward Bill Monroe to get their picture taken with the queen.

"See you on the field," Georgia says, hitting me on the shoulder with her glove as she passes by.

I blush and giggle like a little girl. Tom is shaking his head. I pull myself together.

"It doesn't matter," I tell them both. "I'm through with love."

"That's what they all say," Raven sighs.

Beach Avenue

The Aquatic Centre always reminds me of days off with Mom. We'd splash around for hours while she taught me how to swim. It was just the two of us. I had her all to myself. I savoured every moment of it. But what I loved most about swimming at the Aquatic Centre was the mural in the hall leading to the men's change room. It was painted in the seventies and had lots of oranges and avocado greens. The artist was clearly inspired by the 1976 Olympics and those old ParticipACTION ads. The mural offered me a rare glimpse of a body builder wearing a pair of posing briefs and is clearly based on Arnold Schwarzenegger. He was my first crush.

Here and now, the swimming competition is clearly the place to be. Everyone outside the Centre looks like they're from Central Casting. Everywhere I look it's Tom Cruise and Jodie Foster. I try to buy a ticket to get in, but it's sold out! Now what am I going to do?

"Hey, Dwayne," Mary Brookes says. "Here to check out the boys in Speedos?"

"I was going to, but there's no tickets left," I say.

"This was one of the only events that sold out." Mary winks at me and says, "Follow me."

We walk past the ticket takers without them even batting an eye.

"Have fun looking at all the boys," Mary says, and goes back out the glass door.

The skylights fill the Centre with sunshine. If it wasn't for the humidity, I'd swear I was still outside. Sometimes when I was a kid, I'd float on my back and stare up at the sky pretending I was in the middle of the ocean. But now is not the time for nostalgia. I have to find Tom. I squint and look around to see if I can find him. It's loud with cheering. All the guys are cruising. I feel so unattractive in my black shorts and shirt. It's like I bought a ticket to see The Cure only to find out it was for a Belinda Carlisle concert.

"Dwayne!"

It's Lawrence, another volunteer. We spent a lot of time together this last year stuffing envelopes and entering names into a computer. He's in his fifties. He works for the government or something. He never did give me a straight answer when I asked, like he didn't want me to know.

"Hey, Lawrence," I say, giving him a hug. "You volunteering?"

"Are you kidding?" he says, his eyes going from one good looking man in a Speedo to another. "I wouldn't miss this for the world. How about you?"

"Spectator," I say, looking for Tom's face in the crowd without trying to be obvious about it.

"Did you see the editorial in *The Sun* on Wednesday?"

"The one where they basically took back every horrible thing they said about the Games for the last four years?" I say. "I saw it."

"I tacked it to the bulletin board in the lunch room at work and invited my co-workers to come to the Games." His voice catches. "Never in my wildest dreams did I ever think I would come out at work. I always assumed I'd get fired."

It's weird to think how far we've come since I've been alive. The West End can be a bubble as far being gay goes. You can be who you want as long you do it between Davie, Denman, Robson, and Burrard Streets.

My nostrils flare.

"Do you smell Calvin Klein's Obsession for Men?" I ask Lawrence.

"All I smell is chlorine and suntan lotion," he says.

I inhale once more through my nose and catch the scent. It's moving through the crowd toward the bleacher seats.

"I just saw the friend I was meeting," I say. "I'm going to be volunteering at Celebration Centre a few times this week. Maybe I'll see you there."

I work my way through the crowd. From the top of the stairs I can see Kent stepping over knees to take the seat Tom is saving for him. Kent presses a cold can of Coke against Tom's arm. I can feel the sexual tension from here. God, I wish that Tom looked at me like he's looking at Kent right now.

I should go home. Instead I go down the cement stairs, trying not to step on the people watching the competition. I excuse myself as I make my way down the row where they're sitting, pretending like I'm just coming back from the bathroom, as if I've been here the whole time.

"Hey, you two!" I say.

Both of their smiles fade a little when they see me. My heart sinks. Tom inhales deeply, as if a spell has been broken.

"Dwayne!" Tom says. "You remember Kent from registration."

"We ran into each other this morning," Kent says. "Imagine seeing you here."

"Kent's friend might break the world record in the butterfly," Tom says.

"We're just teammates; we both swim on the same team," Kent corrects. "He swims in the Masters category. He just turned fifty but has the body of a man half his age."

"It's still pretty cool," Tom says.

"I didn't know people still called things *cool*," Kent says, elbowing Tom. I try to look away, but I can't. "There's Mike now. I think this it."

The swimmers take their places. It feels like everyone in the bleachers is leaning forward. The Aquatic Centre is silent for the first time since I got here. The starting whistle sounds and the swimmers dive into the pool, launching themselves forward with arms wide as wings, pellets of water coming off their fingers like they're in slow motion. I'm surprised the skylights aren't shaking from all the cheering. The race is over in under a couple of minutes. There's a pause while the timekeepers post the times.

RRAAHHHHHHWWWWW!

Everyone in the Aquatic Centre is cheering.

"He did it!" Kent shouts over the noise. "He broke a world a record!"

Kent hugs Tom and lifts him off his feet. Tom looks confused. Confused and excited at the same time. Kind of how I imagined my face looked when I discovered masturbation for the first time.

"That was incredible!" I say. "I'm so glad I was here to see that."

Kent looks at me, annoyed. Tom looks like he wishes I'd go away.

"Now that that's over, I think I'll go back to my hotel for a little disco nap," Kent says. "Would you like to come?"

"I'm supposed to go the opening of Words Without Borders," I say.

Kent glares at me.

"Tom," Kent says. "Would you like to come back with me to my hotel and have a disco nap?"

"What's a disco nap?" he asks.

"It's a nap you take before clubbing," I say.

"Maybe for you it is," Kent says, a twinkle in his eye.

Tom doesn't look so sure of himself anymore. He pulls back from Kent slightly. He's obviously tempted but nervous. It's not because of me though. He's still questioning.

"I'm going to hang out a bit longer," Tom says.

Kent can't believe what he's hearing. I think this could be the first time he's been turned down by a man. I'm glad I was here to see it. That means he will only try harder next time.

"Suit yourself," Kent says. "If you want to get a hold of me I'm at the Landmark Hotel on Robson."

Tom watches Kent make his way back up the cement stairs.

"I think I need to go cool off in the ocean," Tom says.

"I'll come!" I say, getting up from my seat.

"I thought you said you were going to some big opening."

"I have time."

"I don't know," Tom says, rubbing his neck. "I wouldn't mind being alone for a bit."

Tom looks like he's trying to make up his mind about what to do. Like's he's considering ditching me and catching up with Kent. But then it's like the old Tom kicks in, the one that isn't hot to trot for Kent. I can feel the tension in the air ease.

"We should see if Gina is doing anything," he says. "I'm dying to find out what happened with the pitcher from Boston."

Denman Street

The line to get into the WESA T-Dance at the West End Community Centre is long, but is moving quickly.

Everyone who was on the ball field is here. I say hi to about twenty people I know, their cheeks, neck, and forearms burned. The auditorium where we came for registration is now a dance floor. I'm surprised to see as many women as there are men. I start to circle the dance floor, then decide to go back and get a drink from the bar. I run chest first into the person behind me.

"Sorry, I wasn't looking where I was going," I say.

"Gina?"

It's her. It's Georgia. She's wearing the *Nobody Knows I'm Gay* shirt she bought the day we met at Little Sisters.

"Hey, Georgia."

I have no idea what to say next. And apparently neither does she because we're both just standing here. "Everybody Everybody" ends and the DJ plays "Wallflower Waltz" by k.d. lang.

"Want to dance?" I ask her.

"I'd like that a lot."

Almost every woman in the auditorium walks out onto the dance floor to slow dance. There's a few guys in cowboy boots and hats, but it's mostly the lesbians. Georgia rests her head against my shoulder and my heart floats. I've been trying so hard to get over Timbre. I forgot how it feels to be close to someone.

"How did your games go to today?" she asks me.

"We won all three," I tell her. "That means we won't have to play tomorrow during Pride. How about you?"

"We lost one which means we'll be missing the parade," she says. "Don't dare cheer because we lost."

"I'd never do that," I say, even though I secretly yelped when she told me.

"I feel like I should tell you," Georgia starts to say. Here it comes. She has a girlfriend back home. "My coach doesn't want us getting romantically involved with the other players until after the tournament is over."

"Your coach doesn't or you don't?" I ask her.

"No. We got lectured about it over breakfast this morning," she says. "But I agree. We came here to win."

"Then what are we doing dancing?"

"I wanted to be the first in line for when the tournament is over," she says. "Do you think you can wait that long?"

"My friends don't think I should be getting involved with a member of an opposing team as well," I tell her.

"And you don't care?"

"Oh I care. I want a medal as much as you do," I tell her. "But I'm recovering from a broken heart. I want to put that behind me as much as I want gold."

The song ends. I take a step away so I can look at her.

"Let's just be friends until the tournament ends, okay?" Georgia says. "I don't want to be responsible for another broken heart."

"What makes you think you will be?" I ask her.

"Let's just play it safe for both our sakes," she says,

avoiding the question. Georgia gives me a quick peck on the lips and runs off.

Now I'm really turned on. I get out of the auditorium as fast as I can to catch my breath. I need to cool off so I walk toward English Bay.

"Gina!" Tom shouts from the water as I come down the cement stairs at Bikini Beach.

The tide is high. There are small clusters of heads dancing on the waves. I strip down to my bra and underwear and swim out to where Tom and Dwayne are treading water. Something is off between them.

"How was the tournament?" Tom asks.

"Won every game," I say. "How were the boys in Speedos?"

Neither of them says anything.

"Someone broke a world record," Dwayne says.

"Cool!"

The sound of the waves serves as conversation. We continue wading in silence, letting the ocean have its way with us, our faces pointed toward the horizon, taking in the day.

Monday, August 6, 1990
Gay Pride Day

Pacific Street

"Dwayne!" Mom shouts down the stairs.

"I'm in the kitchen!"

"I was afraid you might've already gone out with your friends," she says. "Stay there until I get out of the shower."

I'm flipping through *Entertainment Weekly* while I eat a bowl of Raisin Bran with banana. The jungle beat of house music rattles the kitchen walls. I feel like I'm in a *Tarzan* movie. The music is coming from Sunset Beach. The Pride Parade ends there, not far from our place. It's like this every year.

"Why aren't you dressed?" Mom says, coming down the stairs. I can smell her Herbal Essences shampoo from here. A pink feather boa is draped around her neck. It's like this every year.

"I'm not volunteering for, like, another couple of hours," I say.

"What about the parade?" she says, shaking the ends of her boa at me.

"You've seen one Pride Parade, you've seen them all."

"Little Miss Jaded," Mom says. "It's tradition! Like Thanksgiving!"

"I hardly think oiled go-go boys are anything like Thanksgiving."

"Turkeys are basted in oil!" Mom says. "Why are you pouting? You love Pride Day!"

I can tell Mom anything. But she always wants to give advice. She's always reminding me she was a Fag Hag back in the day — her words, not mine. Like this makes her the perfect mother to a raise a gay son. Which it probably does. But some days all I want is to say what's on my mind without the lesson after.

Screw it. I need to vent.

"Everyone's so damn good-looking!" I say. "I used to feel ugly when it was regular Pride, but now with the Games, it's Pride on steroids. Literally!"

"Baby, who's telling you you're ugly? I'll show them what ugly is."

"They don't have to say it," I tell her. "I went to the beach with Tom and Gina last night. Every guy we passed checked Tom out. He's so used to it he doesn't even notice. If I glance in anyone's direction, they look away."

Mom stage-slaps me across the face and shakes my shoulders.

"Snap out of it!" she says, impersonating Cher. It's her schtick. "So what if your friend is attractive? That doesn't mean there's less love in the world for you."

"I just want to be seen. Is that so much to ask?"

"I see you," she says, pinching my cheeks. "If a man doesn't see you, then he's not the one. Trust me. That's how I ended up with you."

I take back what I said about the advice. Mom had me young enough to remember how it feels to be my age. She knows what she's talking about.

"It's these magazines," Mom says, tapping my *Entertainment Weekly*. "They make you feel bad about yourself so you'll buy things."

"It's a list of the one hundred best movies," I say, holding up the cover for her to see.

"Talk to the hand," Mom says, putting her palm to my face. "Now put on your clothes. I have a parade to cheer for."

We amble down the hill to Beach Avenue. Mom takes my hand like when I was kid. It's the one thing I haven't grown out of. I doubt I ever will.

We take our usual spot under the trees at the corner of Bute and Beach. I can hear the Dykes on Bikes in the distance. The revving of their engines always makes my hair stand on end. I start to feel less sorry for myself.

A couple of guys bump into me as they walk past. Each has a muscular arm draped over the other's shoulders. Both are wearing low-cut tank tops, micro shorts, and fanny packs. Outfits purchased at D&R Clothing, no doubt. All they sell is spandex. The one closest to me turns as if to apologize. It's the manager from Fluevog. He recognizes me and looks away.

Second Beach Pool

I can hear Uncle Fred pant as his head breaks the surface of the water. His form is all wrong. He doesn't pace himself. And his Speedo is still way too small. It'd take a year to get him swimming at an intermediate level, never mind an international competition. He slaps his hand against the white edge of the pool. I tap the Lap/Split button on my watch.

"Three minutes, ten seconds," I say.

"Is that good?" Uncle Fred says, panting.

"That depends on the number of swimmers in your division who have never competed before."

"Who am I kidding? I can't do this! I'll be laughed out of the pool."

"But you won't!" I tell him. "I was there yesterday. They cheer for everybody! It doesn't matter what place you come in."

"I feel like I'm drowning half the time."

Now Uncle Fred is making excuses. If I don't give him a pep talk he might bail on the competition entirely. "You're panicking because you think you're running out of air and you think you're running out of air because you have poor form and you're wasting your energy."

I can see the frustration on my uncle's face. I've been in his shoes. It took weeks of practice to learn how to do the egg-beater kick so I could keep my arms above the water to throw the ball. I can still see Dad's stern face looking down at me, telling me to act like a man. But that's not going to work with Uncle Fred. Now that I know the real reason Uncle Fred is competing in the Games, I have to make sure he sees it through to the end.

"You know it's okay to want to win right?" I say.

"What do you mean?"

"If there are enough swimmers in your division that are slower than you — and based on what I saw yesterday that's entirely possible — you could actually get to the podium."

"Did you say podium? As in medal?"

Uncle Fred looks to the clear blue sky as if he never considered this before. He's imagining standing on a podium, bending forward to receive his medal. I know that look. Athletes do it all the time.

"Tell me more," Uncle Fred says.

"You need to learn to save something for the home stretch," I tell him. "If you let me, I can teach you how to glide just below the surface of the water with the least amount of effort."

"When you put it that way," Uncle Fred says. "Okay Tom, I'll put my faith in your capable hands."

No one's ever called me capable before. I just hope I'm not leading him on by letting him think he can win a medal. But like dad says, "Delusion is often the path to victory."

Commercial Drive

I squeeze a dollop of hair gel into my palm. The smell reminds me of the salons Mom used to take me to so I'd look like a girl. I use the gel to sculpt my sausage curls into a mullet. I still look like Kristy McNichol in *Little Darlings*. I'm going to need a bigger tube of gel.

"Still hiding your dyke hair from your mom, Gina?" Rhonda, my fast pitch coach, says as she enters the bathroom at Josephine's Cafe.

"I'm easing her into it," I tell her.

Rhonda goes into a stall and lights a cigarette. "Head's up! Timbre's just arrived with Cerise."

"*My* Timbre?"

"How many Timbres are there?"

"But it's Pride Day!" I say.

"Welcome to the world, Baby Girl." The toilet flushes.

I poke my head out the door. Timbre is sitting in the window with her guitar case and Cerise. A baby dyke is already buzzing around their table like a fly at a picnic. She's no doubt reminding Timbre she's the next k.d. lang. As if Timbre needs reminding.

It was only a couple of weeks ago that I was sitting in Cerise's Doc Martens. I'd smile and nod like Cerise is now, pretending I didn't want the person to go away. That's the burden of dating the most popular lesbian folk singer in Vancouver. I must not have pretended enough because along came Cerise. Or, to be more precise, Timbre came to see me play softball and got to third base with second base at the BBQ after the game.

"You make a better wall than a window," Rhonda says, trying to get past me.

"Sorry."

I go back out into the cafe, pretending not to see them as I make my way to the door. I'm almost free when …

"Gina!"

Curse Timbre and her sexy raspy voice. She sounds like Carly Simon and Alannah Myles rolled into one. How can someone who shattered my heart so thoroughly still make me weak in the knees?

"Hey, Timbre," I say, acting butch and failing miserably. Cerise is smiling like she's happy to see me. Bitch.

"Did you hear I'm going to be playing at the Gayla!

A Celebration of Women's Culture concert at the Orpheum?" Timbre asks.

"I saw your name on the poster," I say. "No photo though."

This has the desired effect. Even Cerice's face whitens a little.

"There's some pretty big names on the line up," Timbre says. "Kate Clinton. Farron. I'm lucky to be playing the Orpheum this early in my career."

"Oh my God! Raven's here," I say. "She's driving me to the parade."

"Where?" Timbre says. "I don't see Raven."

I slip out the door as fast as I can and round the corner. The sidewalk is overflowing with dykes. I had planned on spending the day here and enjoying the scene. Best to cut my losses and head downtown. The last thing I need is Timbre's friends throwing shade at me.

I hoof it to Commercial/Broadway Station. The SkyTrain can't come fast enough. I'm practically doing a two-step waiting for it to arrive. The car is packed with people. I haven't seen the SkyTrain this busy since Expo. All the passengers are happy and smiling like it's Mardi Gras. The locals are talking to the athletes asking what sport they play and where they're from. At every stop someone shouts, "Have a good Games," as they leave the train. People were never this happy during Expo. It's kind of sad that I feel more comfortable on the train than I do in my own neighbourhood. Love ruins everything.

Second Beach Pool

We spread out our towels and rub ourselves down with sunscreen. The sun bleaches the cement pool deck white. It feels like we're in Greece. Kids scream with laughter as they zip down the slide. Moms shelter paper baskets of French fries from the seagulls. The drumbeat of the Pride Parade thumps across English Bay.

"All these men secretly eying each other makes me feel like I'm in a *James Bond* movie," Uncle Fred says.

"What do you mean?" I ask.

"Come on, Tom, even you know what cruising is," he says. "You're getting checked out every which way. I don't know if I should be proud or jealous."

I sit up on my towel and look around. Amongst the families and leathery seniors are toned, tanned men playing connect the dots with their eyes. Some of them are checking me out. I'd be lying if I said I wasn't turned on a little. But I honestly don't know what to do. I've imagined what it's like to make out with a professional athlete or a movie star. I've even imagined what it would be like to make out with one of my teammates. Not once did I ever imagine what it would be like to meet a complete stranger for sex. It's more than I can handle. I lie back down on my towel, my aviators pointed to the sky. Uncle Fred starts laughing.

"What's so funny?" I ask.

"You! You're such a Mary Ann Singleton."

"What's that's supposed to mean?"

"You're a prude," he says. "You know how you were saying it's okay to want to win? Well, it's also okay to want to have sex. As long as you're safe!"

"What do you expect me to do? Just walk up to some guy and ask them if they want to go back to their place?"

"Yes! But cruise them first to make sure they're interested," he says. "Make eye contact with someone, and when they look back, smile."

"Now?"

"Yes now!"

I sit up on my towel and look around. I feel kind of guilty checking out other guys when Kent has been going out of his way to get to know me. It's not long before I meet eyes with a guy across the pool. My first impulse is to look away, but I force myself to keep my eyes on his. I smile. The man sits up straighter and smiles back. He lifts his sunglasses for a better look and raises his eyebrows. The possibility that I could have sex with this guy scares and excites me at the same time.

"I need to cool off," I say. I dive into the pool before things get too serious between me and the stranger.

"No diving!" the lifeguard shouts through his blowhorn when I surface again.

"Tom got in trouble, Tom got in trouble," Uncle Fred

teases, wading toward me in the pool. "Cold feet?"

"I don't know if I'm ready for this Uncle Fred," I say.

"You will be when the time is right," he says. "But we should probably go. I think your friend over there is expecting a happy ending."

We get out of the pool and gather our things. I look over at the guy I was checking out. He's still staring at me. Now I really feel bad. We can't get through the turnstile out of the pool area fast enough.

"Does my family ever talk about me?" Uncle Fred wonders out loud, as we walk past the Fish House in Stanley Park on our way back home.

"Sometimes at Thanksgiving or Christmas," I say. "Like when they remember something funny that happened."

"So before I came out," he says. "Figures. I could cure cancer and all they would remember about me is that I'm gay."

"Why did you stop coming home to visit?"

"Because I'd spend all that money and five hours on a plane to be ignored. No one ever offered to pick me up at the airport or a place to stay. But they always expected me there."

"Because we're your family."

"They're not my family. Gaetan, Raven, my clients at legal aid. They are my family."

Is this what I have to look forward to if I come out?

I'm pretty sure Mom could handle it. But Dad ... I don't know if he would ever look at me the same again. I don't know if I'm ready to risk that. All this, the West End, the Gay Games, Second Beach pool! It's like a movie. It's magical, but it's not reality. Not my reality, anyway.

"Why aren't you at the parade?" I ask Uncle Fred.

"You've seen one, you've seen them all," he says.

"Bill Monroe said that we have to go to every parade no matter what, or they'll take it away."

"He said that now, did he?" Uncle Fred sighs. "Then I guess we're dropping off our things and going to the parade."

Plaza of Nations

"It still feels like the BC Pavilion," Lawrence says, looking around the glass-covered Plaza of Nations.

"No one speaks of pavilions anymore, and that saddens me," I say, quoting Sandra Bernhard's *Without You I'm Nothing* album.

"Did you come here for Expo, Dwayne?" Lawrence asks.

"Yeah. I saw enough wholesome family entertainment to last me a lifetime."

"Most of the performers were gay. A friend of mine slept with a theatre student from Toronto."

"And now that same stage is playing host to every gay choir, band, and chorus from across the globe," I say.

124

"Serves them right for trying to hide us from the tourists," Lawrence scoffs.

Today is the first day of Celebration Centre, where, as well as live entertainment and the Art Market, athletes and visitors can get all their information and official merchandise. Tonight is the first night of the big dance party at Enterprise Hall, the glass box on the waterfront. I'm dying to go. I wonder if I can talk Tom and Gina into it.

I'm straightening the pamphlets and programs on the table when someone says, "You bastard."

"Do you know this person?" Lawrence says indignantly.

"He's my manager at A&B Sound," I say.

Justice is dressed like a black hole. His shoes boost him up couple of inches so that he's towering over me. He's holding a black umbrella to protect his black-and-white makeup from the sun.

"That's no excuse for that sort of language!" Lawrence says.

"He stood me up!" Justice says, pointing at me. "I bought him a ticket to an event and he stood me up! Probably so he could spend time with that closet case!"

"Dwayne? Is that you?" someone else asks.

I look across the plaza and see Warren from school. My first crush that wasn't a mural or celebrity. Can this Pride Day get any worse?

"Hey, Warren," I say, trying to drum up some enthusiasm.

"Are you a volunteer here?" Warren asks.

"He's a traitor, that's what he is," Justice says, stomping away in his Frankenstein shoes.

"I almost didn't recognize you in primary colours," Warren says, pointing at my blue volunteer shirt. "How have you been? What have you been up to?"

"This," I say, gesturing at the plaza. "I've been hanging out with some cool friends. Tom and Gina. Tom's roommate gave us VIP passes to Celebrities. We go all the time."

"You've been clubbing?" he asks skeptically.

"Totally," I say. I pull out the VIP pass to show him. "We don't get carded or anything. It's like a gay get-out-of-jail free card."

Warren turns the card over in his fingers, impressed.

"You still with Louise?" I ask, regretting it the moment the words leave my lips.

"Yeah. She doesn't feel comfortable coming here. I saw the editorial in the paper and thought I would check it out."

"What do you think?"

"Not what I expected," he says.

"What did you expect? Drag races and swishing competitions?" Lawrence says from his plastic chair.

Warren thinks about it and says, "Yeah. I did. Kind of. I should get going. I got a job bussing tables at The Keg Coal Harbour."

"I always saw you as a Le Château kind of guy," I tell him.

"People change, Dwayne," he says. "Have a good Games."

I watch Warren walk away. I don't know if I'm over him yet, but it was good to see him, even if he's still dating that bitch, Louise.

"Styles may change, the technology might get better," Lawrence says, "but teenagers will always remain the same."

Sunset Beach

I lose Uncle Fred almost as soon as we get to Sunset Beach. One minute he's saying hi to some friend and the next minute he's gone. I walk through the crowd, secretly checking out guys from behind my aviators. Everywhere I look it's one handsome man after another. I've had enough girls follow me home from school to know that I'm attractive, but here I feel like an ugly step sister.

I make eye contact with a guy wearing a toga. His pecs cast shadows over his torso. Hair perfect, barely smiling, he looks like he should be selling aftershave. Our eyes lock, and the world around us vanishes ... only to be replaced by another pair of eyes, and another. I feel like I'm swinging from tree to tree in a jungle with each glance. My ass is pinched. Knowing hellos are made.

I feel like I'm losing my balance. I want to grab onto someone, but I don't know who.

"Where have you been all my life?" a smooth voice asks. It's Kent grinning from ear to ear. "Imagine running into you in a crowd of a thousand men."

"I'm looking for my uncle," I say.

"I don't know about an uncle, but if you play your cards right I'm sure you can find a Daddy."

I'm kind of turned on, even though I don't get what Kent is trying to say. I take Uncle Fred's advice and stare right into Kent's eyes. His gaze is intense, like he's wearing those X-Ray glasses they sell in the back of comic books. I've never been so attracted to someone before. I look away.

"What do you say we go back to my hotel and grab something to eat?"

"Hotel?" I stammer.

"Yeah. It's a tall building with rooms to rent for the night."

What am I waiting for? Even if we do have sex now, nobody will ever have to know. But what if I go back to his place and we get naked and I freak out and panic? What if we start to kiss and I realize this whole adventure was one big mistake? Worse, what if we do have sex and he gives me AIDS?

"As long as it's only food," I say.

Kent looks a little hurt at first, but then he raises his

eyebrows and smiles like a lighthouse in a storm. He holds up two fingers and says, "Scout's honour."

Davie Street

I'm lost in a remix of "I Am What I Am" by Gloria Gaynor on the dance floor at Celebrities. I've never been a huge fan of disco and house music. The only time I ever dance at a lesbian bar is when someone asks me, and it's usually a country song.

I dropped by Fred's place to see if Tom was home. Gaetan said he was out with his Uncle, but invited me in to hang out with him and their billet, Kouri. I'm pretty sure Gaetan and Kouri have been getting it on. Both of them were wearing nothing but swim trunks and glued at the hip. More power to them. At least someone is getting some action. It was Gaetan who suggested I come to Celebrities to take my mind off Timbre and Georgia.

"Celebrities throws open the doors at two," he told me in that cute French accent of his.

So here I am, clapping my hands to gay anthems, one right after another.

"Gina!"

I recognize Dwayne's voice over the music. I stop dancing long enough to give him a hug. It feels good. I think he needs one as much as I do.

"Happy Pride!" I shout.

"Is it?" he asks. "Three people threw shade at me today. Three!"

"I ran into Timbre and Cerise on The Drive," I shout over the music. "I've been shell-shocked ever since."

"I caught a bit of Timbre's act on the main stage at Plaza of Nations," Dwayne says. "I don't get the appeal. She's just a haircut playing a guitar."

I pick Dwayne up in my arms and swing him around in a circle.

"Thank you for saying that," I tell him. "Even if you're lying!"

"I'm not," he says. "I'm getting bored of every lesbian singer/songwriter trying to become the next Indigo Girls."

"Do you mind if we go upstairs for a bit?" I ask. "I'm starting to feel like a crushed tomato."

"Lead the way."

The second floor of Celebrities is a narrow balcony where you can look down at the dance floor. It's a great way to get from one side of the bar to the other when it's crowded. We find a spot to rest and catch our breath from dancing. I test the railing before I lean against it to make sure it isn't wobbly. Celebrities is the oldest dance hall in the city. It started out as a dance academy when it opened at the turn of the century and then became a ballroom for rich people. In the sixties it was a hippy bar. It became a gay club in the seventies. As I watch the dancers below, I imagine the gay people who came here when the place first opened in the Edwardian era, longing to dance with someone of the same sex. I wish they could see it now.

"I can hardly feel my legs," I say, wiping sweat from my forehead. "I need to save my energy for tomorrow."

"Mom says dancing takes your mind off your problems," Dwayne says.

"And what are your problems?"

The neon lasers bounce off Dwayne's face as he looks down on the dance floor.

"I'm in love with Tom," he says.

"I thought you were going to say you're a virgin."

"Is it that obvious?" he asks me. "Do you think he knows?"

"He hasn't said anything to me."

"Should I tell him?"

"No!" I say.

"You could have hesitated!"

"I'm doing you a favour," I tell him. "Tom is what Raven would call a hopeless situation. It's what she said about Timbre. And she was right. I wished I'd listened to her."

"How is Tom a hopeless situation?"

"He's still poking his head out of the closet," I say. "Plus he's obviously in love with this Kent guy that he keeps talking about. You'll be getting in the way.

Timbre's friend Tiffany is totally in love with Timbre. Always hanging around expecting Timbre to see the light. It's not a good look."

Dwayne looks disappointed. I hate bumming him out on Pride Day, but he needs to hear it.

"This isn't the first time this has happened," Dwayne says. "I fell in love with my best friend at school. He said he was straight, but I didn't believe him. And then he started dating this girl, Louise. I tried to break them up, and when that didn't work I told him it was either her or me, and he chose her."

"The vagina is a powerful drug," I say.

"You're telling me."

"I get it, though," I say. "After Timbre dumped me for Cerise, I was positive I could make her fall back in love with me again. All I did was make an idiot of myself."

"I wish I knew how to make myself stop feeling this way for Tom."

"You can love him without having sex with him," I say. "Besides, the three of us have been having such a good time these last couple of weeks. Do you really want to risk losing that?"

"No," he says. "This is already the best summer of my life."

The opening notes of "Groove Is in the Heart" start up. The whole club screams its approval. Dwayne grabs my hand we run back down the stairs to the dance floor.

It only takes us a couple of beats to become one with the music again.

Robson Street

"Look at all the people on the beach, Kent," I say, gazing out across the West End. Our table was facing the Harbour when we were seated. I barely noticed the restaurant was rotating until the sun got in my eyes. "This view is amazing."

"They don't call it Cloud Nine for nothing," Kent says.

"If you put a revolving restaurant in Mississauga, all you'd see is smoke stacks and factories."

The sidewalks are crawling with people. Not just the main streets. I can see parties on balconies, lost balloons floating out to sea and rainbow flags hanging out of windows. This is what it must have been like when World War II ended.

Kent holds up the bottle of wine he's been drinking, offering me some. I shake my head no. I can't count how many Friday and Saturday nights I've spent trying to buy booze with my friends, and now I'm turning it down. But I need to be in control. I like Kent a lot. I want to touch his chest and arms. I want to know what it feels like to have his arms around me. Following my instincts is hard enough without this stupid disease hanging over my head.

Kent puts his hand on mine. I flinch a little. If he

notices, he doesn't say anything. I shouldn't be so uptight. Every table in the restaurant is a same-sex couple.

"I really have to hand it to Richard Dopson and the board for pulling this thing off," Kent says. "When they announced the Games were coming to Vancouver, I was sure it would be a disaster. It nearly was."

"What do you mean?"

"They didn't have any money," Kent says, rubbing the top of my hand lightly with his fingers. It feels nice. "The government wouldn't give them any grants. They couldn't get a loan from the bank. They nearly lost all their venues because they couldn't pay the balance on the deposits."

"So where did they get the money?"

"Richard and his friends called every wealthy person they knew, and they called two friends, and they called two friends, and so on and so on ... like the Faberge Organics shampoo commercial," Kent says. "Pretty much every wealthy homo from around the globe kicked in a few thousand bucks to make it happen. They're still fundraising as we speak. The proceeds from the party at the Plaza of Nations is going right back into the Games."

I return Kent's grip on my hand and look into his eyes. As a Canadian, it bugs me that he didn't think Vancouver had what it took to host the Games. But those eyes, that face, distracts me from all that. The way his shirt clings to his shoulders and chest. I've never had permission to look at another guy like this before. I've always been sneaking glances. I wonder what my father would think of me now, and the spell is broken.

"I love that everyone is so comfortable being gay in public, but what happens when the Games are over?" I ask. "What happens after the flame goes out and everybody goes back to their hometowns? How will they be able to hide who they are knowing what the world could be like?"

"You make it sound like a bad thing," Kent says. "You don't need a bullhorn or to drape yourself in a rainbow flag to be gay. I prefer the discretion."

"But I thought the Games was about visibility," I say.

"I'd rather be comfortable than visible," Kent says. "I'll be fine whether we have gay rights or not. Just as long as I don't get AIDS. I'm here for a good time, not to change the world."

"Harsh," I tell him.

"Tom, you have all the ingredients to be like me," Kent says. "You're handsome, you have a solid body, and you're white. The world is your oyster. Being gay is just the icing on the cake."

Kent asks for the cheque.

"What now?" I ask him.

"I send you on your way like I promised."

"That's it?"

"You sound disappointed. Are you?"

"Maybe. A little."

"Good. Remember that for next time."

I go with Kent back to his hotel room. We stand outside the door and he squeezes my arms, feeling the muscles in my forearms and biceps. We hug and it feels so good, so natural. If he invited me in I'd say yes. But I'm still too afraid to ask him myself. He kisses me politely on the forehead before slapping me on the butt and gently pushing me down the hall in the direction of the elevators.

I think about what Kent said about gay rights as I walk back to Uncle Fred's house. His attitude about the Games is the exact opposite of what my uncle has been telling me. Kent can put down gay activists all he wants, but if it wasn't for them, the Games could have never happened.

Uncle Fred is sitting on the front steps of the house when I get there. There's a party going on inside the house and in the backyard. I crack open the gate and sit down next to him.

"Where have you been?" Uncle Fred asks.

"Having dinner at a revolving restaurant with a rich and handsome American."

"You've come a long way, baby!"

"Why you aren't inside enjoying the party?"

"I got overwhelmed. I was pouring myself a drink and looking around at all my friends when I remembered the friends who aren't here. Troy, Vince, Michael … they were looking forward to the Games as much as anyone. It made me wonder why I'm here and they're not."

"Are you okay?" I ask. "Can I get you some water or a drink or something?"

"Don't mind me," he says. "I'm just being drunk and maudlin. You should go inside. Gina and Dwayne just got here. They're looking for you."

"I'd rather stay here with you, if you don't mind."

"Suit yourself."

I hear Uncle Fred suck back the tears. I have no idea what to say to comfort him, so I put my arm around him until he rests his head on my shoulder. We watch the people on the sidewalk going by. "Happy Pride," they shout to us. Strangers all of them, but today everyone is our friend.

Tuesday, August 7, 1990

Bute Street

I'm the first to wake up. Uncle Fred is lying on his back, sweating vodka. Out in the hall, I can hear Kouri snoring in the spare room. I walk softly down the stairs to start the coffee. While the coffee brews I go out to the front porch to collect the papers. I'm startled by the sight of two guys asleep on the front porch. Not knowing what to do, I grab the papers and slink back inside the house.

Back in the kitchen, I flip through the newspaper. The ink stains my fingertips. I hear the coffee pot gurgle. This is the first time I've been alone since I came to Vancouver. It's so quiet. I forgot what silence sounds like. I flip through the Gay Games official program to see what events are happening today. Lots of readings at the Queer Arts Festival, as Gina insists I call it. There's a Meet & Greet party at the Celebration Centre hosted by Team San Diego. There's a lesbian dance party at the Commodore, and a drag show at the West End Community Centre. I'd love to go to the Meet & Greet but I volunteered to umpire the softball tournament this afternoon after I'm done coaching Uncle Fred at the pool.

The phone rings. I answer before it can wake anyone up. "Hello?"

"Tommy? Is that you?"

I didn't notice how much Dad and Uncle Fred sound alike until now. My first impulse is to say, "Wrong number," but it won't help. Time to face the music.

"Dad?" I ask. I stand close to the phone in case someone comes down and hears our conversation.

"Hey, sport," he says. "How's the weather there in Vancouver?"

Dad always asks about the weather when he's trying to avoid talking about feelings. His and mine. And even then, he sounds like he doesn't really want to know.

"Hot," I say. "Really hot." Which, under the circumstances, is probably the wrong thing to say. "Sorry for not calling. It's so amazing here. The beach is a few blocks from Uncle Fred's house. I've gone swimming in the ocean everyday. The people here are so chill. I'm already making friends."

"About that," Dad says hesitantly. "I was watching the news last night, and they were saying something about these gay Olympics going on over there."

"You mean the Gay Games?" I say. "They're nothing. It's like Track & Field Day at school."

"That's not how it looked on TV."

"Vancouver is a small city. Things look bigger on TV than they are in real life. Like the rear-view mirror of a car."

"Did your uncle tell you to come out there?"

"No! I just … I needed a break," I say, searching for the words. And then I say one of the few honest things I've said to my dad in a long time. "I'm not sure who I am, Dad."

"You're a man," Dad says, almost aggressively. "You're my son. Isn't that enough?"

I wish it was. I want to be like everyone else. It's not for lack of trying. At least I have been trying here in Vancouver. If only I had the guts to tell him that. But he wouldn't understand. And I'm not sure I blame him.

"Are you there, Tommy?"

"I'm here. I don't know how to answer your question."

He snorts through his nose like a bull. It's his way of letting me know that he's upset without actually yelling at me. It's how I know to come home when I've stayed too late at a friend's house or when I do a lousy job mowing the lawn. I know he's upset with me, but I wish

I could reach through the phone and hug him. I could use his support right now.

"This conversation is clearly going nowhere," he says. "I don't know what this is all about, but you need to check in with me and your Mom to let us know you're okay."

"Uncle Fred has been keeping an eye out for me."

"That's no comfort to me whatsoever," he says. "I'm letting you go."

It sounds like he's firing me as his son. Like he means forever. I feel adrift. Lost at sea.

"I love you, Dad," I say, trying to smooth things over.

"Fine," he says, and hangs up the phone.

I put the phone back on the cradle. I turn around and see Uncle Fred standing in the doorway of the kitchen wearing a faded old bathrobe.

"I should have known you hadn't called them," he says, and takes his place at the head of the table.

Broadway

I was hoping to sneak in a few extra z's before the tournament starts, but the Alma bus won't let me. Every time I'm about to nod off, the bus comes to a screeching halt and jolts me awake. I made a point of not staying out too late so I'd be fresh for the tournament, but I couldn't fall asleep. Between the Games, Mom, Timbre, and Georgia, I've got too much on my mind.

The bus is packed with gay and lesbian athletes and people on their way to work. A lesbian softball player is standing next to a guy in a business suit who's reading the paper. A bear in spandex is talking to a nurse. It's surreal and perfectly normal at the same time. I'm amazed at how quickly everyone has gotten used to it. For years, the religious right had been threatening us with the fires of hell if the Games went ahead as planned. Today feels like just another Tuesday, but with more mullets and handlebar moustaches.

The bus stops at Broadway and Granville. Most of the business people get off to go downtown to their office jobs, and are replaced with more women's fast pitch players going to Connaught Park for the tournament.

"Morning, stranger," Georgia says, hanging onto the faded yellow safety strap above my seat.

"You're bright and chipper," I tell her. "Shouldn't you be hung over from Pride?"

"I don't drink," she says. "Ironic considering I'm Irish and from Boston. My parents are teetotallers. I don't see any bags under your eyes. What's your excuse?"

"I'm technically not old enough to drink. I only became old enough to participate in the Games a week ago."

"How old is not old enough?"

"Just turned eighteen."

"At least you're legal," she says, laughing. "You in college?"

"Taking a year off," I say. A half-truth. I haven't ruled out university; I just don't know when I'll go. "How about you?"

"U of M Amherst. I'm trying to get into MIT."

"Are you a scientist or something?"

"Something," she says. "You live at home?"

"For the time being. I'm currently in the process of figuring that out. My mom is giving me the distinct impression I've worn out my welcome."

"That sucks," she says. "I'm not out to my parents. We're Catholic. You know how it is."

"Do I ever."

"I'm not really out back home," she says. "My real sport is basketball. I have a shot at making it to the U.S. team for the '94 Olympics."

"I've never met anyone who is aiming for the Olympics," I say.

"I've seen you play ball," Georgia says. "There's no reason why you wouldn't qualify for the Canadian Olympic team. Especially the way you Canadians play."

"Ha-ha," I say. "If basketball is your game, why are you playing softball?"

"Can't risk getting outed," she says. "I've worked too hard to lose my spot over something as silly as being gay. Like that has anything to do with my ability to dribble a ball."

"Right? I didn't realize how uptight I was around straight people until we became the majority."

143

"You don't think less of me do you? For not playing basketball?"

"Not at all," I tell her. "But my friend, Raven, would, so don't mention it to her."

"One of my teammates is on my case about it," she says. "That's why I'm back here with you."

"Sucks that you can't be who you are even in another country.

"America: land of the free, right?" Georgia says. "Just as long as you're straight, white, and male."

She laughs like it's a joke, even though it's true. Not like Canada is any better. The provincial and federal governments didn't hide their disdain for the Games. They wouldn't let us use the tax dollars we pay into to fund the Games because they didn't think they'd "benefit the community." What a joke.

I take a chance and look up into Georgia's face. She's still smiling down at me. I've known her less than a week and she's already been more honest with me than Timbre ever was in the two months we dated. I want to stand up and kiss her. But I know the rules. Plus, if she's not playing basketball to avoid being outed, what else is she hiding?

Granville Street

The only time I've ever been to the Orpheum was when I came here on a class trip to see a matinee of

Swan Lake performed by the Royal Winnipeg Ballet. I remember the hockey jocks complaining it was "gay — like Dwayne." I didn't care for once. If these guys with their huge thighs and wide shoulders were gay, then sign me up.

I didn't blink the entire performance. It wasn't only the men. I was enthralled by the ballerinas as well. The amount of strength it took to prance around the stage on pointe. How they glided through the air like paper airplanes. It opened my eyes to what beauty is.

Ten years later and I'm backstage at the Orpheum, surrounded by muscular men and women pumping up for the preliminaries of the physique competition. Rows of bench presses and racks of dumbbells fill the wings. There are enough mirrors to make it feel like I'm in the funhouse at the PNE. Competitors are rehearsing their routines, flexing and stretching their arms and legs in diagonals to show off every ripple of their muscles. Their skin is tanned. Their hair is perfect. And their posing briefs are tiny.

"Hey, Dwayne," Mary Brookes says, handing me a hot cup of coffee. "You look like you need this."

"Thanks," I say, blowing on the surface to cool it off. "What was I thinking volunteering for this first thing after Pride?"

"I know exactly what you were thinking," Mary says, looking around at all the bodies.

"Did you have a fun Pride?" I ask her.

"I was run off my feet all day," she says. "I've been so busy I've barely had to time to enjoy the Games."

"Then I should be the one getting you a coffee," I say.

"It was on my way," she says. "Some lovely specimens, don't you think?"

"Is it me or are some of these bodies kind of ..."

"Doughy? Leathery?"

"That's one way of describing it."

"All are welcome. Anyone can participate," Mary reminds me. "It's not a body building competition. It's a *physique* competition. You don't need muscles to have a physique."

"I can't get over how confident some of these people are," I say. "There's a guy who is old enough to be my grandfather in nothing but a banana hammock."

"So?"

"I have nightmares of walking out in public looking like that. Why do you think I'm always wearing baggy black clothes?"

"You have a perfectly fine body."

"Then why do I repel people?"

"You're young, funny, and intelligent," she tells me. "You could have anyone you want."

"You don't know what it's like being me."

"Dwayne," Mary says putting her hand on my shoulder, "My parents kicked me out of the house for being gay, and yet somehow I helped organize one of the biggest sporting events in the world this year. I think I have some idea of what it's like to be you."

"I'm sorry," I say.

"Don't apologize to me. Apologize to yourself — that's the one you're hurting." Mary thinks for a moment and says, "I have the perfect job for you today."

"Tell me you need a fluffer."

"Close. But first, are you allergic to baby oil?"

Second Beach Pool

"Why doesn't it feel like I'm moving?" Uncle Fred says, slapping the water with the palm of his hand.

"Because your heels aren't connecting when you kick," I tell him. "And you're wasting energy by taking a breath on every stroke."

"I need to breathe!" Uncle Fred snaps.

We've been practicing for thirty minutes now. In the slow lane. The breaststroke competition is tomorrow. At this point, I'll be happy if I can keep him out of last place. It's not looking good. He either ignores every piece of advice I give him or he refuses to try.

"There's air in your lungs," I say, trying to be patient with him.

"How do you know?"

"Because you're floating."

"Smarty pants," he says under his breath.

"Sass won't make you faster."

"You sound like your father," he says. "It's his fault I'm not good at sports. It didn't matter what sport we were playing, he always made a point of being on the opposite team because he didn't want to lose. Who does that to his own brother?"

I've been waiting for Uncle Fred to blame Dad for his breast stroke. The whole time I've been in Vancouver I've had a hard time believing they're even brothers. Now I can hear them arguing in their room.

"Then this is your chance to prove him wrong, isn't it?" I say, starting to get a little sassy myself. I believe Dwayne's word for it is "attitude."

This gets his attention. Uncle Fred takes a breath and adjusts his Speedos.

"What is it you want me to do again?" he asks.

"Here, let me show you," I say. "Get out of the pool and walk alongside me while I swim."

I push off against the blue wall of the pool and glide through the water. I go as slow as I can so that my uncle can see every movement in the stroke. I can see my shadow on the bottom of the pool. It's what a bird must see as it glides above the beach. Each stroke creates a ripple that is reflected on the concrete below.

There's glory in competition, but there's also peace. The pool is the one place I can shut out the world, tame my thoughts. Whatever is on my mind when I got into the water is quickly forgotten, replaced by my determination to stay afloat, to perfect my stroke so that it becomes second nature, so that I become one with the water. It doesn't happen every practice, but when it does, it's amazing.

"Has anyone told you how beautiful you look when you swim?" Uncle Fred asks.

"If a teammate told me I'm beautiful they'd get called a fag," I tell him.

"What's wrong with the world that a man can't compliment another man without getting verbally assaulted?"

"Hop in the water," I tell him. "I still need to get to the ballpark to umpire women's fast pitch."

It takes a few metres and some handholding, but Uncle Fred finally gets it. He's still taking a breath on every stroke, but at least he's scooping his head below the water's surface instead of dunking it. I get him to do a hundred meters in the slow lane. The first fifty meters he takes his time. He's no Victor Davis, but his stroke is consistent. He's working with the water instead of against it.

The last fifty isn't as good. He's falling back on old habits. I can see him losing confidence. He's thinking about the finish line instead of where he is in the pool. He's panting when he reaches the wall.

"Better," I say. "But you still need to save something for the home stretch."

"I can hardly breathe right now," he says. "But there was a moment when I wasn't thinking about what I was doing. It was like my body took over and my mind went along for the ride."

"It's cool, isn't it?"

"It was amazing."

If nothing else, my uncle got to experience how it feels to be an athlete.

Connaught Park

It's our second game of the day. We beat Team Regina pretty handily, but it was a good game nonetheless. I felt bad knocking another Canadian Team out of the tournament. The Americans have been picking the Canadians off one by one.

Tom is umpiring the game. I like having him here. We have a connection that comes with being queer and playing sports. The playing field is the one place we can hide in plain sight and be ourselves at the same time. Even now, standing behind the catcher, his face hidden behind a cage, it's the happiest I've seen him.

We're playing Team Colorado. They're a tough team. They sing "Rocky Mountain High" whenever they get on base. Our hitters are heavier, but their outfield is strong. Their shortstop has elastic arms that can reach just about every hit that comes her way. I swear to God their left fielder has spring coils on her cleats the way she leaps in the air to catch a ball. The game has been tied for two innings. It's the top of the sixth. Colorado is on deck.

Their first two hitters get on base one right after another. I start to lose my cool. I want to slam my glove onto the gravel, but Rhonda frowns on that kind of thing. "We might be a lesbian team, but we're still ladies," Rhonda would say, which makes no sense to me. You can take a girl out of the fifties, but you can't take the fifties out of the girl, I guess.

I take my position between second and third and focus on the batter in the box. That's when I see Timbre sitting in the stands almost directly behind Tom at home plate.

POP!

A line drive heads right at me. I reach to get the ball, but my glove hits Cerise's like a pair of hockey sticks at a face off. We're able to slow the ball down but it gets past us. The runner on first whips by on her way to third.

"Get back to second!" I shout. Cerise returns to her base. I recover the ball and whip it to third before another runner makes it home. Such a stupid error.

"What were you doing!" I shout at Cerise. "That was my ball!"

"It was closer to me!"

"If you paid more attention to the ball instead of Timbre we could have had a triple play!"

"Funny, from where I was standing it looked you were the one who was paying attention to Timbre."

Raven comes running over to us from the pitcher's mound.

"Girls!" she says, sounding pissed. "We have a game to win. Save the drama for the bar."

I sulk back to my position. When I look back toward home plate, I notice that Timbre is smiling. She's playing me and Cerise like the strings on her guitar, and I have no idea how to stop it. I avoid looking at Timbre and see Georgia watching the game. Please God. Tell me she didn't just see me yell at Cerise.

We manage to keep Colorado to just one run, but I'm annoyed all the same. Hard as I try to concentrate on the game, my mind is overflowing with all the things I want to say to Cerise. But it's not her I'm mad at. It's me. Every time I see Timbre I feel humiliated. And angry at myself for letting her get to me the way she does.

"Gina!" Tom shouts as I'm walking back to the dugout. He raises his thumb at me and says. "You got this!"

It takes us a couple of batters, but we get a runner on base.

"Gina, you're up!" Rhonda shouts. I jog to the front of the bench. Rhonda stops me and says, "Try hitting it low. That outfielder is too good. Do your best to keep the ball away from her glove."

"I'll try."

"And don't pay attention to Timbre," she adds.

"Thanks, no pressure," I say, and jog to the batter's box.

"You okay?" Tom asks.

"No pep talks from the umpire!" the Colorado catcher shouts.

Tom makes a face like he just stepped in dog shit. It's enough to calm me down and get me back in the game.

I ignore the first pitch.

"Strike!" Tom shouts from behind me. I glare at him. He glares back. This is obviously not his first time at the rodeo. That was not a strike. He better not be over-compensating his calls because he's my friend. Or because he's intimidated by the catcher from Colorado.

The next pitch is a beauty. I manage to hit it with the end of the bat. It zooms a foot away from the pitcher and just low enough for second base to miss it. Even the outfielder with the spring-coiled feet has to run to get it. I'm stopped at second but manage to get a runner in and tie the game.

We win the game by a run in the seventh inning. I haven't felt this relieved since I passed my driver's test. After we're done slapping the other team's hands, congratulating them on a good game, I search the stands for Georgia.

"She left with her team already," Tom says from behind me.

"That obvious I was looking for her, huh?"

"Not as obvious as why you made that error in the sixth," he says. "This is why you can't date the other team."

"You're seriously going to lecture me right now?" I ask. "We just won the game."

"Just saying ..." he says.

"Talk to the glove," I say, holding my mitt up to his face. "What's on your gay agenda tonight?"

"I'm keeping an eye on Uncle Fred. He competes tomorrow. I'm worried he's going to try and chicken out. How about you?"

"Lesbian dance party at The Commodore."

"Why do they call it *gay* when it's guys and *lesbian* when it's women. I mean, it's the Gay Games, right?"

"Why do birds suddenly appear whenever you are near?" I say. "I don't know these things. I'm still getting used to saying the world *queer.*"

"You've been hanging out with Dwayne too long," Tom says. "You're starting to talk like him."

Raven is waving her glove over her head in the dugout.

"Last call for a ride home," she shouts to us. Tom and I make our way toward her.

"I got to hand it to you, Gina. You're an excellent shortstop and a heavy hitter," Tom says. "And the ladies love you."

"They're not ladies, they're women," I tell him. "And that strike you called on me was a ball."

"Not from where I was standing," he says.

"Admit it, you were afraid of the catcher."

"Totally," he says. "I was so glad when you hit that ball."

Granville Street

I nearly fainted when Mary told me I'd be rubbing down muscled bodies with baby oil for the better part of the day. One of the event organizers handed me a white towel and a bottle of oil and demonstrated how to shine up the contestants without getting too handsy. I've never even kissed a man before and here I am rubbing oil onto their shoulders, biceps, and thighs. I try to keep my composure. Try not to come off as creepy. Each contestant welcomes my touch. I can feel the energy from their bodies entering mine through the palms of my hands. It's spiritual.

I'm stationed near the entrance to the stage, which is decorated with marble-hued pillars and podiums. Contestants are waiting in line to make their entrance. The Orpheum is at capacity. You can hear it in the applause, the cheers, the oohs and ahs. Flashbulbs ignite like tiny explosions around the theatre. Routines, carefully choreographed as anything by the Royal Ballet of Manitoba, radiate grace and joy and strength. They're like Roman statues posing on their pedestals, returning the gaze of the person looking up at them.

The competition isn't limited to individuals; couples are competing as well — same sex couples as well as mixed. The couples are my favourite because they're not only flexing, but performing a slow-motion dance, working together to make each other look good for the judges. It's gives me a lump in my throat.

There's an intermission while the judges tabulate the final scores. There's nothing left for me to do but go home and commit this night to memory. I hang out in the wings to watch the medal presentation. I don't know when I'll be backstage at the Orpheum again. I want to soak it in for as long as I can. I'm still lost in the magic of the evening when someone taps my shoulder.

"Hello! I'm Richard Dopson!" he says. "I'm going to be presenting the medals. Do you know where I'm supposed to go?"

Richard needs no introduction. It was Richard who asked Tom Waddell if Vancouver could host the Games. It was Richard who spearheaded the Metropolitan Vancouver Arts & Athletics Association who organized and is running the Games. It was Richard who kept the community updated on the Games with his monthly column in *Angles*.

"I'm Dwayne," I say. "Mary told me to tell you to wait right here. The MC will introduce you when the lights go down again. I'd shake your hand, but they're covered in baby oil. I was polishing the competitors."

"Lucky you. I just get to hang medals around their necks. I was at the equestrian event earlier. Not bad for a day's work."

Richard has tight curly hair, a moustache, and a bright smile. He reminds me of a gay Gordon Lightfoot. These past three years I've seen Richard at fundraising events and on TV promoting the Games. This is the first time I've had the chance to speak to him in person.

"I want to thank you for everything you've done," I say. "I still can't believe the Games are actually happening."

"It wasn't easy," he says. "I know not everyone was happy with all the decisions the board made. But every committee has a male and female co-chair. There's near gender parity among the athletes. And because of the Games, Vancouver now has a gay bowling league and a gay film festival. The community really rose to the occasion."

"I can't get over how diverse the city is right now," I tell him.

"That's how I felt when I went to the first Games in San Francisco in '82," he says. "Tom Waddell always said the Games are a reflection of the global community's health, vigour, creativity, and involvement. I don't see a better example of that than here in this theatre. Look at all these healthy bodies. Look how strong we are even with a disease that has cut a swath through our community. And we continue to thrive. They can never keep us down as long as we work together."

The MC stops by to tell Richard they'll be handing out the medals shortly. The lights dim in the theatre, and the MC welcomes the audience back to the show.

"Whatever made you ask Tom Waddell to bring the Games to Vancouver?" I ask him.

Richard shrugs his shoulders and says, "I don't know."

"Ladies and gentlemen, Richard Dopson!" the MC announces. Richard runs out on stage and waves to the audience.

It's nearly eleven by the time I'm done volunteering. I walk out into the open air and stretch. I shake out the bottom of my volunteer t-shirt to let some air in. Crossing the street, I grab a Coke and a Big Mac at McDonald's. I dump my fries into the lid of the container. A hand reaches down and grabs one. I feel threatened at first, but then I look up and see Gina standing at my table.

"You nearly gave me a freaking heart attack," I tell her.

"They're only fries," she says.

"I thought you were some homophobe trying to start a fight."

"Sorry." Gina takes a seat on the plastic bench across from me. "How was the physique competition?"

"Inspiring, surprisingly enough."

"That is surprising."

"How was the lesbian dance at the Commodore?"

"Packed! I've never seen so many women cut loose like that."

"Was your big lesbian crush there?"

"Yeah," Gina says, sounding kind of down. "She was dancing with some other girl. She saw me go off on Cerise today at the tournament. I may have scared her off."

"She's just playing hard to get," I tell her.

"Raven and Tom are right," she says. "It's not a good idea getting involved with Georgia. I mean, I don't know this girl from Eve right?"

I push the Big Mac container closer to her side of the table. "Have a fry. It'll make you feel better."

Gina grabs a handful and shoves them into her mouth. That wasn't what I had in mind, but what are a few fries if it helps take your friend's mind off their troubles?

Wednesday,
August 8, 1990

Bute Street

It's nearly two-thirty in the morning. I'm sitting upright in Uncle Fred's bed, arms across my chest, fuming. I hear the sound of keys scraping against the front door. I run down the stairs and open it. Uncle Fred falls forward onto the hall floor; his house keys slide across the wood. He looks like Superman flying, one arm at his side, the other outstretched in front of him.

"Where were you?" I demand, tapping my foot. "You're competing in less than six hours!"

Uncle Fred rolls over onto his back. I'm amazed he didn't break his nose in the fall.

"Did you know about the dance party at the Plaza of

Nations?" he slurs. "I haven't danced to Donna Summer since the seventies."

"How are you going to swim when you can't even stand?"

"Relax!" he says. "I'll smoke a joint and sleep like log. I'll be as new as good in the morning."

"The morning is only a few hours away!"

"Who's the adult here?" He raises one arm. "Help me up, will you?"

I pull Uncle Fred to his feet and carry him up the stairs to his bedroom. He pulls a small wooden pipe and a plastic bag of weed from his top dresser drawer. He packs the pipe, but is too drunk to light it. Frustrated, I take the lighter away from him and hold the pipe to his lips. I hover the flame over the pipe's well as he takes a few puffs.

"Want some?" he says. "It'll calm you down."

I'm not a fan of inhaling any kind of smoke, but I'm wound up enough to take him up on the offer. I take two long pulls from the pipe and start coughing so hard I think I'm going to throw up.

"Cough to get off!" Uncle Fred says, laughing like a little kid. He crawls under the one white sheet that covers the bed and falls fast asleep. I'm not far behind him.

The alarm goes off at six in the morning. I have to reach over Uncle Fred to hit snooze. I'm groggy from the pot, but its nothing a few cold blasts of Coca Cola won't take care of. Uncle Fred is on his back snoring like a sea lion.

"Wake up, Uncle Fred," I plead. "The competition is in a couple of hours."

"I don't care. Let me die here in a pool of my own vomit."

"You can't be that hungover."

"You don't know me!" he slurs. "You don't know my hangovers!"

There's no way I'm going to let him miss the competition. Time to rally the troops. I throw open Gaetan's bedroom door. He doesn't have any clothes on. And he's not alone.

"Sorry," I say when I see them.

"S'all good," Kouri says, throwing the sheets off himself.

I gasp again.

"Stop clutching your pearls," Kouri says. "Why waste the money going to the clubs to get laid when the hottest man in town is just down the hall?"

"Aww ..." Gaetan says to Kouri adoringly.

"What's the bother?" Kouri grunts.

"It's Uncle Fred. The swimming competition is in a couple of hours. I can't get him out of bed!"

"Leave this to me," Kouri says, getting up. I've never seen so much hair on one person in all my life. "Step aside, kid."

Kouri tromps down the hall like a Sasquatch. I follow him as he goes into Uncle Fred's bedroom and pulls the sheet off my uncle. He takes one of his hands and pulls him up, throwing my uncle over his shoulder like a fireman.

"What are you doing?" Fred protests helplessly. "Let me die! Go on without me!"

Kouri carries Uncle Fred into the bathroom. He drops him in the tub and douses him with cold water from the shower. I look at my uncle, soaking wet in his boxer shorts. He looks like he's melting.

"I gave you a roof over your head," Uncle Fred says to me. "I fed you. I even let you smoke some of my pot. And this is how you repay me?"

"You'll thank me later," I tell him.

"I take back all the nice things I said about you." He pouts, holding up a hand to shield his face from the cold water. "And to think, I was going to put you in my will."

Connaught Park

Today is the semifinals. We managed to get here with only two losses. Not bad, but I'd prefer it if we were undefeated.

My belly is warm with Egg McMuffin and hash browns. Raven is in zen mode, channelling the Goddess of Fast Pitch to bring her strikes. Rhonda is a chain-smoking mess. The atmosphere of the tournament has been supportive, but competitive. The goodwill of the Games has carried over onto the playing field. We root for the other teams, cheer their successes, feel for their losses. But who's kidding who? We all want the gold medal. Our biggest competition has been the Boston Flamingos and the Nova Scotia Rumours. Never underestimate the Maritimes. They gave us Anne of Green Gables, after all.

Our first game isn't until eleven, but Raven wanted to get here early to warm up her arm. My nerves are tingling. I want a medal so bad. I want to show Mom what I'm capable of doing. Not that she cares.

"Know where I can find a Dunkin' Donuts around here?" a thick Boston accent says into my ear. Georgia looks like she just walked out of an ad for an Olivia Cruise. Her blonde hair rests on her shoulders like it was placed there by God.

"There's one across the border in Bellingham," I say.

"I've been to Washington," she says. "All they have there is Starbucks. I prefer to order my drinks in English, thank you. I don't know how they get away with that mermaid's cooch for a logo."

"The guys at school used to finger it for kicks and giggles," I say.

"Boys … they never miss an opportunity to be pigs," she says.

"Tom and Dwayne are okay. But they're gay. At least

Dwayne is. I keep waiting for Tom to see his big gay shadow and go back in the closet for another six weeks."

"I missed you last night at the Commodore," she says.

"I was there. I didn't stay long."

"Too bad. I was saving a dance for you."

"You were not," I say, remembering how she looked when I saw her dancing with that other woman.

"Fine, be that way," she says, sticking her nose in the air like a brat. "But I could have used you. I ran into an old fling from one of the tournaments. She was so drunk. Wouldn't keep her hands off me."

I wonder if Georgia saw me after all, if she's not covering her tracks. And what does she mean, "old fling from one of the tournaments?" Does she rely on these competitions to meet women? And yet I'm relieved just the same.

"There's line dancing at the Lotus tonight if you'll take a rain cheque."

"I have two left feet."

"So do I."

"The blind leading the blind." Georgia looks at something over my shoulder. "Friend of yours?"

I turn around and see Timbre standing behind us. When I turn back to face Georgia, she's already walking away toward her team.

"What's up, Gina?" Timbre says. She's turning on the butch charm. It reminds me of the first time we met at the Lotus. I was just a kid then. That was only a couple of months ago, but I already feel so much older. I feel myself going weak under her spell all the same.

"Timbre," I say, worried that if I say more I'll betray my feelings for her.

"Wanted to wish you luck today," Timbre says. "I know how much this tournament means to you. Cerise says the team wouldn't have made it this far in the tournament if it wasn't for you."

"That was nice of her."

"I think about you a lot," Timbre says.

"You do not."

"Of course I do. Cerise is great, but she's not strong like you are."

"'Cause she's femme, Timbre. That's why you dumped me. Remember?"

"*You* dumped *me*, remember?"

"I'm not one of your groupies," I tell her. Whatever weakness I felt is gone. "You broke my heart."

"Hearts can be mended," Timbre says. It's a line from one of her songs. "Cerise doesn't need to know."

My heart skips a beat. I've wanted to hear Timbre say those words for weeks now. I see Cerise warming up with another teammate. The ball she was about to throw falls out of her hand when she sees me with Timbre.

All Timbre wants is to be the star of the show, and you were stealing her limelight, I remember Raven saying. It's tempting to let Timbre come on to me. I want to torture Cerise just like she tortured me when she was dating Timbre behind my back. But I can't do it. I don't know if it's my Catholic upbringing or if I actually feel some sort of sympathy for Cerise. But like Rizzo in *Grease*, that's a thing I'd never do. Tom was right. I am starting to talk like Dwayne.

"I think you better go cheer your girlfriend on," I tell Timbre.

If looks could kill I'd be burning at the stake. Timbre is not used to hearing "no." It kind of turns me on. If Georgia was here, I'd kiss her passionately just to piss Timbre off. Instead, I go in search of Raven so I can tell her what happened.

Beach Avenue

It's my first full day off of working and volunteering since Opening Ceremonies. Mom's still asleep. I'm eating Raisin Bran and reading *Vanity Fair*. I have a headache from all the perfume samples, but I'm determined to read the latest Dominique Dunne article after I finish this profile of Carrie Fisher. The phone rings.

"Yo!" I say.

"Dwayne! It's Tom. I'm freaking out."

"Did you run out of Daisy Dukes?"

"I'm calling from the Aquatic Centre. The swimming competition starts in fifteen minutes, and Uncle Fred is DBB."

"Huh?"

"Drunk Beyond Belief. Don't they say that out here?'

"Maybe straight guys do," I say.

"Please come to the pool," he says. "I need all the support I can get."

I'm flattered that he called me for help, but a part of me feels like a patsy. Good on Fred for getting drunk before the competition. This I have to see.

"I'll try and get a ticket," I tell him. "I can't stay all day, though. I promised to hang out with Justice after I stood him up at Words Without Borders."

I decide to wear a black tank top to be summery. Lawrence is manning the ticket booth when I get to the Centre. He's wearing a woman's big floppy hat with horn-rimmed glasses. He's the most effeminate man here.

"Hey Lawrence," I say. "You've really let your hair down since the start of the Games."

"When in Rome," he says. "Besides, I love the shade the brim provides. You here to volunteer?"

"Spectator. My friend's drunk uncle is competing today."

Lawrence rips a ticket off the roll and hands it to me with a wink.

"For your service," he says. "Have you been to the dance party at the Plaza of Nations yet?"

"I'm a minor," I remind him.

"Volunteers are working the door. You could look as

old as Fred Savage and still get in. Go dancing. You'll have the time of your life."

"I have tickets to Dancelebration at the Commodore, but I'll try and check it out after," I tell him.

"Have fun," Lawrence says. "And do yourself a favour: go dancing!"

The humidity sucks the life out of me as I enter the Centre. I wave my bolero hat under my pits to keep my deodorant dry. The bleachers are nearly full. I find a space against the railing and lean against it.

I see Tom and Fred on the pool deck. Tom keeps snapping his fingers in front of his uncle's face trying to keep him awake. Fred has a better body than I expected. And he's wearing the tiniest Speedo. I keep hoping they'll look up and see me, but they don't. So much for being an athletic supporter.

"Will the athletes in the fifty-metre breast stroke please take their places," the announcer says through the loud speakers.

I watch as Tom practically carries his uncle to the starting block. He backs away from Fred like he's balancing an egg. This is like watching Lucy and Ethel.

Poor Fred. He looks like a plant that needs a stake to stay upright. The whistle blows for the swimmers to take their marks. Fred looks like he realizes where he is. The whistle blows again and all eight swimmers dive into the pool. Fred is the last off the block. He starts swimming for dear life. Remarkably, he's not the slowest one in the pool. A handful of swimmers are already raising their hands in victory. There are four swimmers left. The crowd is on its feet cheering like it's the Kentucky Derby. Fred is actually leading the pack. He reaches the opposite side of the fifty-metre pool and raises his arms above is head. Then he sinks into the water like a dirty dish. Tom has to fish him out to get him back onto the deck.

That's one heat down. They should give Fred a medal for making it through the rest of them without throwing up in the pool.

I go to the Coke machine for something cold to drink. I crack the can open and drink it outside to cool off. Kent is standing on the sidewalk in front of the Aquatic Centre. He's talking to another equally hot white guy. Narcissus looking at his reflection. Then I see them kiss. Not a peck on the lips, but a full-on James Wilby making out with Rupert Graves in *Maurice* kiss. I'm turned on and I can't stand Kent. The two part ways. I turn my back to Kent as he enters the Aquatic Centre. I wait until the smell of his cologne wafts away before I go back inside myself.

Tom is sitting near the top of the bleachers with his uncle. A towel is draped over Fred's shoulders like a swaddling baby, his wet head resting on Tom's shoulder.

"He okay?" I ask.

"He's asleep," Tom says.

"How many more heats does he have?"

"Two more of the fifty and then two of the hundred."

"For Christ's sake, Tom, put the guy out of his misery. Let him go home."

"I can't. We have to see this through."

"You're not the one swimming."

"He can't give up now,"Tom says, his voice cracking. "He can't! I promised him he's going to finish strong no matter what place he comes in. And I'm keeping my promise."

I've never seen Tom this emotional before. This isn't about a swimming competition. I've been around enough men with HIV to know that Fred isn't competing for a medal. He's competing against the virus.

Fred lets out a long, loud snore. We both laugh at how pathetic he looks. I take a seat on the opposite side of Fred and squeeze his thigh. I put my arm across his shoulder, making a Fred sandwich. My arm touches Tom's, but he doesn't move it, so I leave it there. It feels good. Strong and warm, like him. But it's not sexual. We're just two guys looking out for a friend.

Connaught Park

I'm sunburnt and tired, but we made it to the semifinals! I love it when the twelve of us click like a well-oiled machine. I made catches I never thought possible. The second game was the toughest. A back-and-forth slugfest against Team San Diego. It took two extra innings to decide the winner. It's the only time I ever felt bad for beating another team. It's just another game. But it's the Gay Games. Everyone came from so far to be here.

I don't want to win for just myself, I want to win for Vancouver, to make the city proud. It's rough being an athlete in Canada. We're the only country that didn't win gold at either of the Olympic Games we hosted. And fine, I'd rather have healthcare than bragging rights every four years. But still. There's nothing wrong with being proud of where you're from, flaws and all. It's still home.

I'm lounging in the shade with the team. Some of them are drinking beer, which I'm quietly frowning upon. I don't want us blowing the finals because someone can't see straight.

"Did you hear who we're playing?" Raven tells me.

"Let me guess …" I say.

"The Boston Flamingos," she says, cutting me off. "Hope your crush goes easy on us. She's got a mean arm."

"Georgia doesn't need to go easy on me," I say. "I'm a heavy hitter."

"Just keep the stars out of your eyes when you're in the batter's box."

I pull myself off the grass and head to the crapper to have a moment to myself. Behind the closed door of the stall, I press my fingers to my temples to focus on the game ahead. I can't. I should have known I'd be playing Georgia. Raven is not wrong. Georgia has a killer arm.

Cerise is leaning against the bank of sinks when I come out of the stall. Her arms are crossed. She looks angry. It's the butchest I've seen her. It bugs me that we're at odds over Timbre. We got along great before she ruined everything.

"I know you're sleeping with Timbre," Cerise says.

"Say what?"

"Don't play dumb," she says. "I saw you with her today. And she's been unavailable all week, and when we're together, she's really distant."

"You just described my entire relationship with her," I say.

"Admit it," she says. Tears start welling up in her eyes. I feel sorry for her.

"Cerise, I'd love nothing better than to say I was sleeping with your girlfriend, but I'd be lying. I know what you're going through. I went through it myself when she started seeing you. This is her way of keeping the spotlight on her. Those groupies waiting in the wings for you two to break up ... they all think they're the one Timbre is going to commit to. But it's never going to happen. The line is too long. Now, do you mind? I need to wash my hands."

Cerise storms out of the washroom. I was worried she

might go for my throat. Not that I'd blame her. I splash cold water on my face. Women! If this is what one ex-girlfriend is like, I can't imagine a string of them.

Beach Avenue

"Are you sure you don't want something to eat?" I ask Uncle Fred. "You've got one more heat. I can grab you a burger at the concession stand down by the beach if you want."

"Do you want me to crap my Speedos?" my uncle says. "I haven't eaten meat since Mulroney became prime minister."

Uncle Fred is sober now, but he looks like he's just had his appendix out.

"What happened to Dwayne?" Uncle Fred asks, realizing he's not there.

"He went to check out the Queer Arts Festival with his friend from work," I say. "He wants to meet at the dance party at the Plaza of Nations later."

"You should go," Fred says. "You know Dwayne is in love with you, right?"

"Yeah. I wish he wasn't."

"Why not? He's funny. He's loyal. He would follow you to the ends of the Earth."

"That's a lot of pressure to put on one person. I don't even know what I'm going to do once the Games are over."

"Just don't be a cock tease," Uncle Fred says.

"What's that supposed to mean?"

"Don't lead him on, like you did to that guy at the pool the other day," my uncle says. "It's cruel to get someone all hot and bothered and throw water on it at the last minute. If you're not interested, let him know. He'll hate you at first, but he'll thank you later."

"I don't want him to hate me."

"It's only temporary. I've been in Dwayne's shoes. How do you think Gaetan ended up as my roommate?"

"You were in love with Gaetan?"

"I was in *lust* with Gaetan; I mistook it for love," Uncle Fred says.

"How did you get over it?"

"He never stopped being my friend," he says. "Don't lose that one, Tom. Gina too. Those are the people you want to keep close. No matter where you end up after this, they're the ones you'll find yourself turning to."

The whistle blows, signalling the end of the heat. Uncle Fred's head rolls backward like he's about to die.

"I don't know if I can swim another race. I can't feel my arms and legs."

"I like that feeling," I say. "Dad says it means you've put in a hard day's work."

"He always was a glutton for punishment."

"Uncle Fred, I know you and Dad have your problems, but he's still my dad. Just because I can't talk to him about this," I say, meaning the Games, "doesn't mean I don't love him. He's been a good dad."

"I'm sorry if I offended you."

"You didn't. But I wish Dad was here to see you compete. He'd be proud of you."

"He'd probably cheer for the other swimmers."

"Dad's not like that. He taught me to always cheer for the home team. It's why we're both still Leafs fans."

"You're *both* gluttons for punishment," Uncle Fred says. "Thank you for getting me out of bed. And thanks for getting me into to the pool. I couldn't have done it without you. You're the kind of brother I wish I had."

"The final heat of the hundred-metre breaststroke is next," the announcer says over the PA system. "Swimmers, please come down to the pool."

"That's us," Uncle Fred says, getting to his feet.

We make our way down to the deck. Uncle Fred steps up to the block. He turns, looks back at me, and smiles. The sun from the skylight illuminates his hair like a halo; he stands above me like he's rising into the heavens. I know this is how I will always remember him.

"Don't forget to save something for the home stretch," I tell him. He gives me a thumbs up and lowers his goggles over his eyes.

The judge blows the whistle once for the swimmers to take their marks, and then again to start the race. Uncle Fred dives into the pool. This is by far the fastest he's swam all day. He's actually pulling ahead of people. And then something amazing happens. Uncle Fred swims faster in the home stretch. In a field of eight he finishes fourth. He slaps the wall and raises his arms like Alex Baumann winning gold at the L.A. Olympics. I pull him out of the pool and hug him, getting drenched in the process. And now we wait for the results.

Uncle Fred shivers under his towel as the judges post the times. His times are nowhere near what is needed for a medal. He finishes fifteenth in the men's fifty-metre breaststroke and twenty-first in the one-hundred metre breaststroke, ages thirty-five to thirty-nine.

"That's it?" I say, looking up at the board. "You worked so hard."

"Tommy, you're looking at the board the wrong way," he says. "I came in fifteenth and twenty-first in the *world*."

I think back to when my uncle explained the *Time Is Running Out* ad on his refrigerator, and how he was able to keep smiling in the face of so much oppression. Now I know how. It's all about perception.

"Gentlemen," a smooth voice says. It's Kent. His Speedo is smaller than Uncle Fred's and looks painted on. Both my jaw and my uncle's drop. "Sticking around for the show?"

"What show?" Uncle Fred asks.

"You'll see," Kent says, winking at me as he gets ready for the freestyle finals.

"Was that the handsome American you had dinner with on Pride Day?" Uncle Fred asks. I nod, still speechless from seeing Kent in his Speedo. "Now I understand what's going on with you and Dwayne."

Connaught Park

The sun is directly above the field. My ball cap is drenched with sweat from the day's play. My polyester jersey is itchy. I want to take it off and just play in my sports bra. The dugout is brimming with nervous energy. We stand with our faces pressed against the fence waiting for the coin toss. Rhonda loses. We're first at bat. *Merde*, as Dwayne would say.

I nod at Georgia on the opposite side of the field. She doesn't acknowledge it. She has her game face on. Harsh. Why did I do that? Now I feel vulnerable. Tom was right: women's softball is cutthroat.

Rhonda tries to psych us up before the game. "I know it's hot, and I know all of you want nothing more than a cold beer to cool off, but the gold medal is in our sights," she says, between puffs of her cigarette. "We can do this! We can bring home the gold, not just for us, but for Vancouver! Who's with me?"

All twelve us of us cheer at the top of our lungs. It's answered with a roar from the opposite dugout. I can hear Georgia's voice among them. I can't remember the last time I was this intimidated playing against another softball team.

"Play ball!" the umpire shouts.

It's on.

Georgia strikes out our first batter, and then the second. We manage to get a couple of base hits, but then Georgia strikes out the fifth batter before we can even get someone to third.

The bottom of the second inning doesn't go much better for The Flamingos. They play the bases, hitting line drives, keeping the ball to the ground instead of in the air where we can catch it. With one out they manage to load the bases. The batter on deck hits the ball right to me. I catch it and throw it home before the runner on third can make it home. Phew. That was a tight inning, and there are six more to go.

I'm the first up at bat. I cross myself without even thinking about it. I stopped believing in God ages ago. I don't know if I ever did. A vision of Mom saying the rosary flashes through my mind. I grab a bat and walk toward the box. I tap the bat against my cleats, and take my position. I look Georgia dead in the eye. We are complete strangers to each other.

"Strike!" the umpire calls.

I didn't even see the ball.

The next two pitches are a ball and a strike. I take a step back from the batter's box to collect myself.

"You got this, Gina!" Raven shouts from the dugout. It's all I need to hear.

I take my place in the batter's box and position myself for the next pitch.

CLUNK!

The ball hugs the first base line. First base reaches for it with her glove and misses. I round the base, my eyes on second.

"Foul!"

Damn it!

I jog back toward the dugout.

"Nice hit, sport," Georgia says.

"Georgia," the catcher shouts. "Focus!"

I smile in spite of myself.

"I can take Georgia out with a stray pitch next time she's at bat," Raven says.

"Nah, I'm good. Thanks, Raven."

Raven puts her arm around me like a sister would. And she is my sister. All of my teammates are. Even Cerise got back into my good graces after I saw her crying in the washroom.

The next few innings whip by. It takes Raven and Georgia a handful of batters to rotate the teams on and off the outfield. Everything falls apart in the fifth inning. The Flamingos' first batter hits a home run. The ball nearly lands in the playground on the opposite side of the park. It was a beautiful hit. I jog over to Raven to see how she's doing.

"How did she hit that?" Raven says. "I put a curve on it and everything."

"Relax," I say. "Just close your eyes and think of the Queen."

"I'd rather think of Diana."

"Whatever works."

We manage to hold The Flamingos off for another couple of batters, but they still get a runner on first and second. Georgia's at bat. I wonder if it's too late to take back Raven's offer of hitting her with the ball. Gently.

CLUNK!

The ball goes over Cerise's head. It hits the dirt. Rachel in outfield grabs the ball and throws it to me. I throw it home.

"Safe!" the umpire shouts.

Judy, our catcher throws the ball to third, but her aim is off. It's coming toward me instead. I hold up my glove to catch it, but the ball bounces off the pocket and onto the gravel. I scramble to get it like an idiot. I throw the ball home in time to see Georgia cross the plate. All three runners are jumping for joy. They are treated to a hero's welcome when they return to the dugout.

I slam my glove onto the gravel. Then I kick it. Cerise runs over, picks up my glove, dusts it off and hands it back to me.

"Could have happened to anybody," she says. She slaps me on the shoulder with her glove and jogs back to second.

Raven strikes out the next two batters. Thank God. Back in the dugout, Rhonda tries to raise our spirits with rounds of "Let's go, S.O.S.!" I pray to the Softball Goddess. I conjure every baseball movie I can think of for inspiration:

Field of Dreams, The Natural, Bull Durham. I pretend the last inning didn't happen and that the game is still zero-zero. It works. We gain back two runs. We even manage to shut out The Flamingos in the bottom of the sixth inning.

Georgia strikes out our first two batters at the top of the seventh. I'm at bat. This is the most relaxed I've been the entire tournament. I stride up to the batter's box, tap my cleats with the bat and take my position. I look Georgia right in the eyes and I smile.

CLUNK!

I don't even have to see it to know the ball is going out of the park. I run around the bases and into the arms of my team. I may have just ruined my chances with the most beautiful woman I've ever laid eyes on, but I just scored a home run on the best pitcher in the tournament. But the thrill is short-lived. Georgia strikes out the next batters. We don't even finish the inning. The Flamingos have already won by a run. The best we can hope for is a bronze.

Beach Avenue

Uncle Fred stays to watch the rest of the swimming competition with me. He says he wants to see "The Show" Kent told us about earlier, but I think he wants to know more about Kent.

How did you meet?

What have you two been doing?

Does he know you're seventeen?

He sounds like my dad after I come home late from a party.

"Have you two had sex?"

"Gross!" I say.

"I'm the closest thing you have to a legal guardian," he says. "If you're having sex, I feel like I have a right to know."

"We hugged in front of his hotel room," I say. "I didn't have to pry him off me, if that's what you're worried about."

"I don't have a problem with you having sex with him," Uncle Fred says. "I lost my virginity to someone much older than I was. It's how it works when you're coming out."

"Then why does he bug you and Dwayne so much?"

"How about this," Uncle Fred says. "The next time you're alone with him, ask him if he voted for Reagan."

"What does it matter?"

"Because if he did, it means he put his bottom line ahead of the community," Uncle Fred says. "If some of these rich guys aren't going to fight in the trenches with the rest of us, the least they can do is get out of the way and stop voting against our interests."

Down on the pool deck, Kent and his teammates are getting medals for the relay. It's his second medal of the day. He's waving to the crowd. I wave back, trying to get his attention, and realizing how pointless it is. I feel like one of the girls who come to our water polo games, and asks if we saw them in the stands, like we're not busy concentrating on the game. It's embarrassing.

The competition is barely over when a group of men dressed in yellow dresses enters the pool area from the men's change room. The dresses are decorated with giant daisies, and they have on white stockings and big sunglasses. They walk with purpose around the pool and climb up to the fifty-metre diving platform. Then, one by one, they take turns jumping into the pool feet first. Once all of them are in the water, they perform a synchronized swimming routine. How they are able to stay afloat in those dresses is beyond me.

"What do you think?" Kent says, joining my uncle and me in the bleachers. "Those are the Marlos. They do this after all the big competitions."

"They're amazing," my uncle says.

"I wish Dwayne was here to see this," I shout over the cheering of the crowd.

"Who's Dwayne again?" Kent asks."

"One of his best friends in Vancouver," Uncle Fred answers, as if to remind not only Kent, but me as well.

Next, Bill Monroe enters dressed as Queen Elizabeth to announce the start of the Flamingo Relay Race. Now a whole other set of swimmers, both male and female, enter dressed as mermaids, lobsters, cheerleaders, and

Elvis. The teams of costumed swimmers line up at the blocks on each side of the pool. Bill blows the whistle, and then the first member of the team dives into the pool holding an inflatable flamingo in front of them. The surface of the water becomes covered with feathers and sequins. The pool staff look on in horror, but there's nothing they can do to stop the race. My uncle and I can't stop laughing. This is the craziest thing I've ever seen in my life.

I feel Kent put his arm around me. Sweat forms between his palms and my skin. My knees buckle a little. I notice Uncle Fred looking at us from the corner of his eye. He smiles at the antics going on in the pool, pretending not to notice. I relax and lean in close to Kent. It feels good. Comforting. I slowly put my arm around his waist and kiss his shoulder. My heart feels like it's going to pump through my chest.

"What are you guys doing tonight?" Kent asks.

"Passing out with a joint and a gin and tonic," Uncle Fred says.

"What about you, Tom?" Kent asks. "I have an extra ticket to the Splash Dance at the Science Centre if you want to come. We can go to the party at the Plaza of Nations after."

"Do you mind?" I ask Uncle Fred.

"Be my guest," he says. "Just remember what I told you, Tommy."

Granville Street

I keep checking my watch, trying to figure out how long I have to stay before I can leave Dancelebration and go to the party at the Plaza of Nations. If I were smart, I'd stay here with Justice. The dance performances are amazing. The crowd at the Commodore is way more my scene — art fags and lesbians. People who put on plays, black and white photographers, poets, and performance artists. I have a better chance of meeting a boyfriend here than on some giant dance floor. But I can't quiet the voices in my head. They keep telling me, "Rescue Tom from Kent."

"One gin and tonic with a maraschino cherry," Justice says, handing me my drink. He's been sneaking me alcohol the whole night. I hiccup after the first sip.

"Isn't this incredible?" Justice says. "I just ran in to Daniel Collins. He told me the whole story about taking the photo for the bus ads. Did you know he had to trick the board into using a photo of the guy wearing a Gay Games shirt?"

"How did he do that?"

"He shot a few rolls of film to loosen the models up. Once they relaxed in front of the camera, he had one of them put the Gay Games tank top on. When he developed the film, all the best photos had the tank top in them. What a trip, huh?"

"Totally," I say. "How do you feel about going down

to the party at the Plaza of Nations?"

"What for?"

"A guy I volunteer with says it's really cool."

"Tom?"

"Lawrence. The guy I was with when you read me for filth the other day."

"I knew you would do this!" Justice says. "These are our people, Dwayne! Why go to a place they don't even notice you're alive? Aren't we good enough for you? Aren't *I* good enough for you?"

This hurts more than I thought it would, but it also pisses me off.

"I really hate it when you make me feel less than," I tell him. "I don't need you to make me feel bad about myself. I can do that all on my own."

"I don't want you getting hurt," he says.

"I think you're projecting your insecurities on me."

"Am not," he says, even though he totally is.

"Then let's go to the Plaza of Nations."

The moonlight reflects off of Enterprise Hall when we get to the Plaza of Nations. It's hard to tell where False Creek ends and the glass building begins. The line to get into the dance seems to go on forever, but it's moving. There's almost as many women as there are men. You never see that at a gay club. It's either one or the other. I hope it stays that way after the Games are over, but I doubt it. Most of the guys are wearing low-cut tanks, short-shorts, or some variation of spandex. A group of women are singing "Closer to Fine." I've never seen so many lesbians in one place at one time. This what the Dinah Shore Golf Tournament must be like.

"Dwayne!" Gina is waving her arms. She's by herself near the front of the line. "Where have you been? I've been waiting for you all night."

I feel weird cutting a line this long, but I want to get in before my next birthday. Justice and I take our place next to Gina. The guys behind her are clearly pissed off about it. *C'est la vie.* I've been volunteering my ass off. I deserve something for it.

"Gina, this is my manager, Justice," I say.

"I was also his only friend before you and this guy Tom appeared on the scene," Justice says, with an eye roll.

"Good to meet you," Gina says. "I promise you can have Dwayne on weekends after the Games are over."

"How'd the tournament go?" I ask.

"We play for bronze tomorrow," Gina says. "All my fault. I totally blew an easy play. And to make it worse, we lost to Georgia's team."

"Georgia's the girl Gina has been crushing on all week," I explain to Justice.

"I figured," Justice says.

"Look on the bright side," I say. "Now you can do her."

"That's what I thought," Gina says. "We had plans to go line dancing, but she totally stood me up! Can you believe that? This is the last time I let a woman lead me around by the nose."

"Right," I say sarcastically. Gina can put up a brave front all she wants, but she wants a girlfriend as bad as I want a boyfriend.

"Should you really be out this late if you have a game tomorrow?" Justice asks.

"We don't play until eleven," she says. "I need to dance off the horrible play I made. And Georgia."

"Gina has only just discovered the healing powers of house music," I tell Justice.

"And I don't know where Tom is, so don't even ask," Gina says. Justice stifles a laugh. Asshole.

The line is moving faster than I expected. The bass from the dance floor makes the glass structure vibrate — *ZZT, ZZT, ZZT.* The people near the front of the line are already moving their feet to the beat of the music, even Justice.

"Can you feel that?" I ask Gina.

"Yeah," she says smiling. The stress of the day is disappearing from her face. It's like she's de-aging.

"I Feel Love" by Donna Summer is playing. We both start dancing on the spot. I close my eyes and inhale the music, transported.

The volunteer at the front of the line gestures for us to go down the escalator. We slowly glide downward and are enveloped in flashing coloured lights. Bodies writhe, fan dancers perform hypnotic routines, daisy-chains of shirtless men weave through the crowd lubricated with sweat. We reach the bottom and are absorbed onto the dance floor. "A Little Respect" by Erasure starts to play. The crowd cheers, and before I know it, Justice, Gina, and I are dancing together, our butts and backs rubbing up against the other dancers. I've never been in a crowd of so many people. It's intense, but I feel safe. I see the manager from Fluevog. Instead of looking away, he smiles and blows me a kiss. He must be high.

We dance to about six songs and are spat out on the opposite side of the dance floor. I feel like I've just finished the hundred-metre sprint. We catch our breath, taking in the lights reflected off the water of False Creek until the DJ plays "Everybody Everybody" by Black Box. We're back on the dance floor again. I bump into someone nearly knocking their beer out of their hand. I turn to apologize and see that's it Tom. He's with Kent. They're both shirtless. I was having so much fun dancing, I completely forgot he's the whole reason I'm here.

"Dwayne!" Tom says, hugging me. He's drenched in sweat, and he smells of B.O. And he's drunk. Really drunk. Gina, Tom, and I drink when we hung out, but never DBB, as Tom likes to say. I've been dying for Tom to hug me these last couple of weeks, but not like this.

"This has been the most incredible day of my life!" Tom shouts at the top of his lungs. "I saw a drag show in a pool. Then we went to the most amazing party at Science World with all these hot swimmers, and now we're here! Isn't this incredible? Gina!" Tom says, seeing her for the first time. Tom hugs her. Then he hugs Justice. "I don't know who you are but you look like you need a hug too. Have you met my friend, Kent?" Kent stops scanning the dance floor long enough to nod at us. "We made out on the dance floor," Tom says.

"Are you okay?" Gina shouts over the music. "You seem kind of drunk. And high."

"I gave him the tiniest bump of ecstasy," Kent says. "Nothing to worry about."

"Oh my God!" Tom shouts. "How'd your game go?"

"We're playing for bronze," she says. "It's fine. Hey, I'm going to get some water in you. I want to make sure you're hydrated, okay buddy? You mind, big fella?" she says to Kent.

"He's all yours," he says.

"I need to pee," Justice says.

I just stay where I am, dancing with Kent.

"Looks like you were able push Tom out of the closet," I say to Kent.

"I have that effect on men," Kent says. "My secret is alcohol."

"What about that guy I saw you making out with at the pool today?" I say.

"What about him?"

"Tom is head-over-heels in love with you."

"And you're head-over-heels in love with Tom. You don't think I haven't noticed? It's kind of sad, actually."

"Tom and I are the same age. You're old enough to be his father."

"But you're in different leagues. Do you really think someone like Tom will go out with a queen like you? The only way you're going to get his attention is if you start doing steroids. Face it, kid. In the grand scheme of things, you're a nobody."

Kent turns his back on me and keeps dancing. I stand there not knowing what to do or say. It's like being picked last for gym class on acid. This whole week I've been trying to love myself, to believe that I belong in this community. But everything Kent just said is one more reminder that I could change everything about myself and it would never be enough.

"Dwayne!" Gina says, stopping me in my tracks. Tom is hanging off her, glowing from the ecstasy. Justice is with them. "We need to get Tom home. I don't like that guy he's with."

"Kent?" Tom says. "Kent is fine. Why don't you guys just leave him alone?"

"Maybe because he gave a minor ecstasy?" Justice says.

"It was just a tiny bit," Tom says, trying to show us how much between his thumb and index finger.

"You know what your friend Kent just said to me?" I tell Tom. "He said I'm a nobody."

"He did not," Tom says. "You're just jealous because you have a crush on me."

The dance floor is hotter than hell, but a chill goes up my spine. Gina and Justice look at each other. Neither of them know what to say. But I do.

"When we first started hanging out you told me that I was safe as long as you were around. Do you remember that, Tom?" I say. "Well, I don't feel safe. In fact, I feel the exact opposite. You lied to me, Tom. You're a liar and I never want to see you again."

I make my way through the crowd as fast as I can, taking the escalator two steps up at a time. I get into the first cab that I can find. I keep my face pointed toward the window, trying not to let the driver see me cry. What made me think the Gay Games would be any different than any other day of my life?

Thursday, August 9, 1990

Bute Street

Uncle Fred shakes me. My head is throbbing. I feel like I've been in a coma. I'm usually the designated driver back home. I'm not used to hangovers.

"Time to get up," Uncle Fred says. "It's Kouri's last day."

I want to go back to sleep, but I'd never forgive myself if I didn't say a proper goodbye. I'm also curious to see what pattern Kouri is wearing for his last day in Canada. I sit up in the bed and pull the sheet up over me.

"Where's my underwear?" I ask.

"You're asking me?" my uncle says. "Gina and some guy I never met had to drag you up the stairs to get you into bed. Now get your Daisy Dukes on and get to the kitchen."

The table is covered with plates of pastries from Maple

Leaf Bakery. A small mountain of bacon is dripping grease onto a paper towel on a plate next to a big bowl of fruit salad. Gaetan is stirring scrambled eggs in a skillet. Kouri is seated at the head of the table like a king. His shirt and shorts are covered with mermaids. He is slurping a cup of coffee when I enter the kitchen.

"There he is!" Kouri says. He gets up from the table and wraps his arms around me in a big bear hug. I can feel my breath leaving my body.

"I didn't want you to leave without saying goodbye," I say.

"Like there was a chance of that." He chuckles. I'm going to miss his pirate laugh.

"One last time," Gaetan says. "What's on the gay agenda today?"

Kouri spreads open the copy of *Angles*. It's been his Bible these last four days.

"There's a drag show at The Commodore," he says. "The men's chorus is performing at the Main Stage at Celebration Centre; there's a women's dance party from six to ten at the Plaza of Nations — that ought to be fun — and Eight Madonnas and a Dick at Graceland."

"What's that?" Gaetan asks.

"Eight Madonna impersonators with stripper Richard Richards," Kouri reads.

"That makes perfect sense," Uncle Fred says.

"Dwayne would love that," I say. "I'd ask him to go,

195

but I don't think he ever wants to see me again."

"Please tell me you didn't get into a fight over the handsome American," my uncle says.

"Okay, I won't tell you," I say. "When do you get back to Australia?" I ask Kouri, changing the subject.

"I'm going to San Francisco first, and then Los Angeles," he says, his mouth full of food. "Got to make these trips to North America count."

"And I'm going to use some of the money I made this week to see Kouri in L.A. for one last fling," Gaetan says.

"Well, isn't that sweet," Uncle Fred says. "I knew you guys were shacking up, but I didn't know it was serious."

"Did I tell you he can lift me over his head?" Gaetan says.

"And I thought the quickest way to man's heart was through his stomach," says Uncle Fred. "No wonder I'm still single."

"Time I got me a cab," Kouri says, looking at the watch on his furry wrist.

"Don't be ridiculous," Uncle Fred says. "Let Tom drive you to the airport."

"I don't want to be a bother," Kouri protests.

"I insist," I say half-heartedly, even though I'd rather go back to bed.

I wait for Kouri by the gate while Gaetan and my uncle say their final goodbyes. My uncle gives Kouri a copy of *The Young in One Another's Arms* by Jane Rule. Gaetan gives Kouri a hard-on.

As we drive across the Burrard Bridge, Kouri takes one last look at the West End, its mid-rise buildings outlined against the backdrop of the mountains. Small whitecaps lap against the shore of Sunset Beach. Tiny ferries crisscross between the Aquatic Centre and Granville Island.

"Amazing how quick a place becomes home," Kouri says.

"Right? These have been the most amazing weeks of my life, and I won't even be able tell anyone when I go back to Mississauga."

"Then don't go back," Kouri says.

"Are you kidding?" I say. "I'm seventeen! My life is in Mississauga. My friends are there. I have a whole other year of high school before I can graduate. I can't run away forever."

"So it's back in the closet for you then, eh?"

"I haven't decided yet," I say. "I kissed a guy last night, but I still can't bring myself to say the words."

"Rip the band-aid off, I say," Kouri says.

I get onto Granville Street and follow the signs to the airport. When I pull up to the departures area to let Kouri out, he leans across the front seat and shakes my shoulders.

"You're a good kid, you," he growls. "I've been in your shoes. The longer you hide from yourself, the more miserable you'll be."

He grabs his suitcase from the flatbed of the El Camino and waves one last time before entering the airport. I watch him disappear behind the sliding glass door. I'm startled by someone honking their horn behind me.

I watch the city come back into view as I drive across the Granville Bridge back into the city. It's small compared to Toronto. The skyline isn't nearly as high. There are mountains instead of skyscrapers. I've never known what it's like to live near the ocean, and now that I have, I'm not sure I want to go back to living without it. I see the exit for Beach Avenue. I merge onto the off ramp, knowing what I have to do.

Pacific Avenue

It's nearly eleven in the morning, and I haven't gotten out of bed. "The Winner Takes It All" by ABBA is playing on my stereo. I stare at my posters of Madonna, Janet Jackson, and Robert Smith. I wish I were them right now, making music videos, touring the world, playing to audiences of thousands of adoring fans. Nothing seems fair. Not even the sun coming up in the morning.

The doorbell rings. I hear Mom go and get it.

"So you're the Tom that did ecstasy and made Dwayne feel like a used Kleenex," I hear her say. "I haven't been able to get him out of bed all morning!"

I run down the stairs in sweatpants and a shirt before Mom says something I'll regret.

"Mom! It's okay," I say. Tom is standing on the landing. If nothing else he looks as terrible as I feel.

"I come in peace," Tom says, holding two fingers up in a V.

"Is it okay if Tom comes in?" I ask Mom. She gives him the evil eye and steps aside to let him into the house.

"Even your pajamas are black," Tom says, following me to my room.

"Now is not the time to comment on my pajamas."

I stand against my desk, my arms crossed, trying to look as stern as possible even though deep down, I can't believe he's here. He closes the door behind him and looks around like Brad Majors entering Frank N. Furter's mansion.

"I had no idea you were so organized," he says. "I've never seen so many records and cassettes in one room."

"The perks of working at A&B Sound," I say dismissively. "I'm surprised to see you. I thought you'd be dressed in one of Kent's shirts having breakfast by the pool."

"Stop it, Dwayne," he says. "That's not fair."

"You came here to lecture me about fair?" If I was flattered before, now I'm just pissed. "You have no idea what it's like to be rejected, do you? You never even experienced homophobia until you had to walk past the protestors outside the community centre a week ago."

"That's not true," he says. "Why do you think I ran away? I once told a guy on the water polo team I liked a girl's dress, and I was called Jeanne Beker for months! I didn't even know who she was!"

"Even you must have seen *Fashion Television*," I say.

"It doesn't matter!" he says. "If I act feminine, even the slightest bit, I'm made to feel like a fag. I feel like I'm trapped in one of those boxes magicians put knives through. I can wiggle my fingers and toes, but I can't move while I keep getting stabbed."

"But you can pass for straight without even trying," I remind him. "That's the ideal gay man. You're respectable. I'm gay as all hell and ugly as sin."

"You're not ugly," Tom says.

"I'm not attractive like you," I say. "Sometimes I wonder why you even hang out with me. You could be friends with anybody in the city right now."

"Are you being serious?" Tom says. "You and Gina are the coolest people I've ever hung out with. Gina shoots from the hip. But you ... remember the Pride party at Uncle Fred's? I went to the bathroom and you didn't see me, but when I came back downstairs I watched you dancing by yourself to some disco song. You looked so happy and free. And I thought, all I want is to be as comfortable with myself as that guy."

It's the nicest thing anyone who's not Mom has ever said to me.

"I just wish you liked me the way you like Kent," I say.

"I wish I liked you the way I like Kent sometimes

too," he says. "It would make things so much easier. But I can't make myself feel something I don't. You've said as much yourself when you talk about your friend Justice."

He got me there.

"Are you going to have sex with Kent?" I ask.

"Probably," he says. "Can you handle that?"

"No, but I guess I only have to put up with him for a couple more days," I say. "What are you doing now?"

"I was planning on going home to sleep. Why?"

"Gina's bronze medal game starts in less than an hour."

Tom's head falls between his shoulders like he can't keep it up anymore.

"I guess we'd be pretty shitty friends if we didn't go watch her play," he says.

"You don't have to."

"Of course I have to," he says. "You have to cheer for the home team, right?"

"How do I know?" I tell him. "I've never cheered for anything before in my life."

Connaught Park

I'd be lying if I didn't say I was a little spooked after I dropped the ball yesterday. We should have this game in the bag, but there's no sure things in a tournament like this. We're playing Team Seattle. We're evenly matched, which makes me a little more nervous. This could go either way.

"Gina!"

I look and see Tom and Dwayne coming toward me. I'm surprised to see them together after last night. I'm not even sure what happened. It all went down so fast. Dwayne's bolero hat shades his eyes. The only speck of colour on him is a pair of red horn-rimmed sunglasses and his yellow Sony Walkman. Even with aviators on, Tom looks like he just left the bar. He's smiling all the same. I'm touched they'd come out to see me play. No one in my family did.

"Looks like you guys kissed and made up," I say.

"We made up," Dwayne says. "Let's leave it at that."

I hug them both, one in each arm. I've never had friends like these guys before. It's so ... uncomplicated. There's nothing sexual between us. All we have to be is there for each other. It reminds me of Raven's relationship with Tom's Uncle Fred. How they're always so happy to see each other. It's what I wished for on my birthday.

"Gina!" Rhonda shouts from the diamond. "The game's about to start."

"I gotta go!" I say.

"Give them hell," Tom says.

"And don't come home without a medal," Dwayne shouts after me.

"No pressure," I shout back as I jog to the dugout and wait with the team for the coin toss.

"Is that Dwayne and Tom?" Raven asks.

"Yeah."

"Good on them," she says. "It's nice to see the boys supporting the girls."

"They're good guys."

"Fred and I have raised you all well," Raven says, smiling to herself.

"Yes you did."

"You hear about Cerise?" Raven says. "Timbre dumped her last night."

I look down at Cerise at the end of the bench. She looks sullen. I want to go over to her and welcome her to the club, but I'm sure I'm the last person she wants to talk to right now. I wouldn't if I were her.

Rhonda cheers when she wins the coin toss. We're in the outfield for the first inning. Maybe the Goddess of Softball is on our side after all.

The sun is already high in the sky beating down on the diamond. You could fry an egg on first base. I must have an inch of lotion on the back of my neck, but I still want more. The dust kicks up as soon as the first batter runs for first and is tagged out. I feel gritty all over.

The first inning is scoreless, but we take a one-run lead in the second inning. We go back and forth for the next couple of innings. Seattle takes the lead by one. Then we take the lead by a run. Cerise is at bat at the top of the fourth inning. Raven is on first. I'm on second. Cerise seems unsure of herself. She steps away from the batter's box to give herself a minute.

"You've got this, Cerise!" I shout.

"C'mon, Cerise!" Raven, cheers.

Soon the entire bench is chanting "Cerise, Cerise, Cerise!"

She takes her place in the batter's box. A swing and a miss. She cocks the bat back behind her shoulder for the next pitch.

CLUNK!

A line drive right past first base.

The dugout is on its feet. I can see Tom and Dwayne jumping up and down, screaming at the top of their lungs as I round third and sprint for home. Cerise is already gaining on Raven, who is not the fastest runner. They both aim for home. Each of them run into my arms. Despite their best efforts and some close calls, Team Seattle never catches up. We win the game by two runs. It's not a gold medal, but at least we're bringing home the bronze. And in this competition, that's nothing to sneeze at.

"Good game, good game, good game," we say, slapping the hands of the opposing team as we leave the diamond. They are disappointed, but not sad. It was an amazing tournament. One that won't be repeated for another four years. But now that it's over comes the realization that my role as an athlete in the Gay Games is over. After the medals are handed out, I'll go back to the deli counter at Santa Barbara, calling out numbers and slicing cold cuts.

We collect our things from the dugout and make our way toward the beer keg. Tom and Dwayne are already waiting for me.

"Congratulations!" Dwayne says. "I'm so proud of you!"

"Did you even know what was going on?" I ask him.

"Of course I did!" Dwayne says. "After Tom explained it to me."

"He was only interested in the uniforms," Tom says. These guys. They're polar opposites, but they go together like Bert and Ernie and Laurel and Hardy.

Tom and Dwayne hang out for a bit after the game. I introduce them to the team and the gals welcome them as one of their own. Some of my teammates are enjoying their company so much I get a little territorial.

"You might want to protect your gays," Raven says. "You don't want Cerise walking off with them like she did Timbre."

That's all I need to hear.

"So, are you two planning on hanging around for the medals ceremony?" I say, putting my arms around both their shoulders and steering them away from the team.

"I should get going," Tom says. "I don't want to fall asleep at the wheel."

"I think I've had enough sports for one day," Dwayne says. "What's on your gay agenda?"

"There's a women's dance at the Plaza of Nations

from six to ten tonight," I say. "I figured I'd go and show off my medal. What about you two?"

"No plans," Tom says. "To be honest, I'd like to stay in. Between volunteering and going out I could sleep until Closing Ceremonies."

"I'm kind of beat myself," Dwayne says. "Last night took a lot out of me."

"Thanks again for coming," I say. "It meant a lot to me."

I watch them as they walk toward the parking lot. They look like a pair of little kids going home from the playground. It's sweet. But there's no chance in hell those two are staying in tonight.

Bute Street

The air feels like honey even with the El Camino's windows rolled down. My tank top looks like I'm a contestant in a wet t-shirt contest. I can smell the plastic from the dashboard as its warmed by the sun. Dwayne is waving his bolero hat in front of his face to cool off. I find a parking spot in front of Uncle Fred's house. I can sense Dwayne lingering behind me as I walk toward the gate.

"Want to come in for a bit?" I ask him.

"Do you mind?"

"I'm going to crash, but you're more than welcome to hang out if you like."

"I've got nothing else to do."

We stagger up the stairs and into the house. Inside the temperature feels ten degrees hotter and it smells like chocolate. The fans in the living room are the only breeze. Gaetan comes down the stairs in the shortest Adidas shorts I've ever seen and a Mitsou t-shirt cropped at the midsection, exposing his six-pack abs.

"*Merde*," Dwayne says under his breath when he sees him.

"*Bonjour*, gentlemen. I'm off to the beach to soak up what's left of the boys," he says. "Care to join?"

"I need to lie down," I say.

"Me too," says Dwayne.

"More for me then," he says, fastening his fanny pack around his waist. "I made some brownies. They're on the table in the kitchen. Help yourself. But save some for your uncle."

I'm starving. Dwayne follows me into the kitchen. A mixing bowl and utensils are drying on the counter. The oven is still cooling down. The smell of butter and cocoa fills the air. I go to the fridge and pour us both a big glass of milk. Dwayne helps himself to a brownie on the plate. He holds it up to his nose.

"Is there pot in these?" Dwayne asks.

I take a slice of brownie and hold it to my nose. I smell chocolate and something else. I shrug and take a bite. Right away I can taste something that isn't chocolate. I wash the first bite down with a couple of sips of milk and take another bite.

"Here goes nothing," Dwayne says, and chomps into a brownie. We both help ourselves to second helpings.

"Want to lie in front of the fans for a bit?" I ask.

"I'm down."

We each take a fan. I can feel my stomach turning from the milk and the brownies. I lie down on the floor. The hard wood feels cold against my sweaty tank top. I close my eyes expecting to pass right out, but nothing happens. My mind bounces from Kent to the softball game to the drive home to the brownies and back to Kent in his Speedos. When I open my eyes again, I'm staring up at the ceiling. I never noticed the details in the trim around the ceiling light before. It reminds me of Kool Whip. How old is this house? I wonder if it's haunted.

"I'm pretty sure those brownies are loaded," Dwayne says.

"I think so too," I say. "Have you ever been high before?"

"No. Have you?"

"I took a hit off my uncle's pipe the night before."

"Maybe we're not even high. Maybe we just think we're high."

"Like when they give you a sugar pill?" I say.

"A placebo? Something like that."

I try to sit up, but I feel glued to the floor.

"I'm either high or having a stroke," I say. "Now what? I can't sleep now. I'm sure as hell not going out on the street in this condition."

"I've got just the thing," Dwayne says.

From the corner of my eye, I watch Dwayne roll over onto his hands. He pulls a cassette out of his man-bag and then crawls over to the stereo. He presses the rewind button on the player. The whir of the cassette sounds louder than normal.

"Do you know who Sandra Bernhard is?" Dwayne asks.

"She like a singer or something?"

"Comedian. She's on David Letterman all the time. She was in *King of Comedy* with Robert De Niro and Jerry Lewis."

"I don't know who you're talking about," I say. "I never know who you're talking about."

"She used to be friends with Madonna until Madonna stabbed her in the back. She's gay or at least bi. You'll love her."

The cassette comes to an abrupt stop. I hear Dwayne press the play button. He crawls back beside me. I hear the fans blowing. Piano music plays. A woman starts telling a live audience about an audition she went to. The way she speaks reminds me of Dwayne. When she sings, her voice is off key.

"What are we listening to again?" I ask.

"*Without You I'm Nothing*," Dwayne says. "It's about to get good."

For the next ninety minutes we listen to Sandra whoever talk about Christmas with the Jensons, going to a gay bar in the seventies, post-apocalyptic white trash, and going to the 1964 World's Fair in 1963.

"There must have been dust on those mints," Dwayne says along with the cassette, and then laughs hysterically.

Maybe it's because of the brownies or because I'm really tired, but I think it's the funniest album in the world, even though I don't get most of it. I look over at Dwayne lying next to me, and he smiles at me with love in his eyes. I'm worried that he's forgotten everything we talked about this morning in his room. But the feeling passes. There's a bond between us I can't explain. I knew it from the moment he asked me, "Are you lost?" I smile back at him, happy to experience what it feels like to love another guy without being ashamed about it. I pull Dwayne closer to me. I kiss him on the forehead, and we cuddle until the album ends.

Connaught Park

I stick around Connaught Park to watch the gold medal game between Team Boston and Team Nova Scotia. I'm totally cheering for Team Nova Scotia after Georgia stood me up last night for line dancing. I've had a couple of beers and I'm feeling good. Raven is making sure I stay hydrated. She's spinning at the women's dance party at the Plaza of Nations tonight. She's expecting to see me there with my medal on.

The teams are evenly matched. It's another nail-biter,

but Boston takes an early lead and manages to hold it. Nova Scotia loses by two runs. They're so happy with silver, you'd think they won gold. That's sports in Canada for you.

Betty Baxter hands out the medals. I look into her eyes as she hangs my medal around my neck, hoping she'll notice me. "Congratulations," she says. I want to lean over and kiss her, but something tells me she wouldn't appreciate that.

I look over at Raven. She's crying, and then I start crying, and before I know it, the whole team is crying. We gather in a group hug. The release of emotions is incredible.

I pretend not to see Georgia when Team Boston is awarded their gold. As soon as the last medal is presented, a keg is cracked open, red plastic cups are handed around, and the field becomes a lesbian bar. Sloppy make-out sessions pop up all around me. I find myself alone in the crowd holding a beer. Raven is off somewhere, hitting on some femme.

"Good game today," a thick Boston accent says to me.

Georgia's cap is on backward. Her cheeks are red with sun. Her blond hair is sweaty and sticks to her neck. She looks beautiful even when she's exhausted.

"Where were you last night?" I say without thinking. "I waited for over an hour and you never showed up."

"I'm sorry, I really am," she says. "Our coach wanted

211

us to turn in early to make sure we were rested for the game."

"So did ours, but I still showed up!" I hate being this cold, but after the way Timbre treated me, it feels good to stand up for myself.

"I choked, okay?" Georgia says. "Flirting is one thing, but going all the way is another. I don't want to get too attached with only two days left of the Games."

"What do you mean attached?"

"You know what I mean. I'm a good Catholic girl. I've been with three women my entire life! What if I fall for you? What happens two days from now after Closing Ceremonies? What then?"

"You think you could fall for me?"

"What do you think has been going on the last few days?" she says. "What are you, stupid?"

The word *stupid* stuns me like a softball to the head. Georgia looks as shocked as I feel. Then she starts to laugh.

"I'm sorry," she says. "I'm really terrible at being a lesbian."

"So am I," I say. I know I should let sleeping dogs lie, but I ask, "How about we go on a date tonight?"

"I'm going to the women's dance at Celebration Centre with my teammates."

"Me too. Save me a dance for real this time," I say. Georgia hugs me and gives me a quick peck on the lips. Stars circle my head.

"It's a date," she says. "I'm going to go before I say or

212

do something stupid to ruin the moment. I'll see you at the dance."

Georgia runs off to be with her team. A thick arm is draped across my shoulder. Five chipped fingernails dangle below my chin.

"Did I chase her off?" Raven asks.

"Naw. We have plans to meet at the dance."

"Ooh," Raven squeals like a teenage girl. "Are you going to buy her a corsage?"

"How would you like it if I poured this beer all over your tits?"

"I don't want to turn the girls on," Raven says. "Let's get back to the city. I need a disco nap before I start spinning."

We're both quiet on the drive home, listening to top ten hits on the radio. It's the middle of August, but I can already feel September creeping up on us. It reminds me of the last weeks of summer vacation before going back to school. I'd spend weeks trying to reinvent myself for the new semester.

"Do you mind going with me to Nick's Barbershop?" I say.

"You want to go to my barber?"

"Yeah. I do."

"Are you ready for that?" Raven asks. "I'll take you wherever you want, but there's no going back from a haircut. Unless you start wearing a wig."

"It's time," I say.

"All right, then," Raven says, slapping my thigh with her hand. "And remember, no matter what happens, you always have a home."

Raven doesn't need to remind me of this. Today is the first time I'm ready to take her up on the offer.

Bute Street

I wake up to the sound of my own snoring. I look down and see Dwayne's head resting on my chest, my arm around his shoulder. The needle on the record player scratches dead wax. My arm is asleep. I want to shake it awake, but I don't want to startle Dwayne. He wakes up suddenly, taking a deep breath like he's just coming through water.

"Where am I?" Dwayne says, looking around.

"My Uncle Fred's. You okay?"

"I feel like there's Vaseline on my eyes. What time is it?"

"The clock on the stereo says it's almost four."

"I always wondered why they put clocks on everything," Dwayne says. "Turns out it's for stoners."

"I'm hungry."

"Me too."

We go back to the kitchen and rummage for food. There are enough leftovers from Kouri's going away breakfast to fill our guts and get us back to feeling like ourselves again. Dwayne eyes the brownies on the table.

"Should we?" I ask. "It was kind of fun."

"I will if you will."

I pull the cellophane off the plate, and we each help ourselves to another square of brownie. Dwayne digs out a cassette of *Like a Prayer* from his man purse and puts it in the player. He turns up the stereo and claps his hands above his head as Madonna sings "Respect Yourself." We both start dancing in the living room.

"You go, girl!" a passerby shouts from the sidewalk.

"Whoo!" Dwayne hollers back. "Have you ever done drag?"

"Like wearing women's clothes? I wouldn't even dress like this back home."

"Want to give it a shot?" Dwayne asks.

I stop dancing. I feel my shoulders tense up. It's like he just asked to see my dick.

"No!" I say, feeling sober all of a sudden.

"It's just clothes. No one will see."

I feel like Dwayne's testing me. Like, if I don't do this he's going to think less of me. I don't know why I care, but I don't want to disappoint him. Especially after last night.

"My uncle has a tickle trunk in his room," I tell Dwayne. "It's where he keeps all his costumes."

"Lead the way!"

We race up the stairs to my uncle's bedroom. I throw open the trunk, and we start digging through the clothes, shoes, and wigs. I hold up a dress for Dwayne to see.

"What do you think?" I ask.

"Very Joni Mitchell," Dwayne says. "And so not you! Here, try these on."

Dwayne throws a denim miniskirt and tube top at me. I strip down to my Jockeys. I see Dwayne trying not to look. A week ago this would have made me uncomfortable, but now it's like dressing up for Halloween. Like Uncle Fred said, I need to keep reminding Dwayne I'm his friend no matter what. I squeeze into the skirt and top.

"Now I know what the inside of a hot dog feels like," I say. "How do women wear this stuff?"

"Wait till you try on the heels." Dwayne dangles a pair of high heels by the straps for me to try on.

"That's where I draw the line," I say.

"Bock bock bock," Dwayne says, imitating a chicken.

"Give me those," I say.

"You closet cases are so easy to manipulate," he says.

I sit on the bed to put on the shoes. Turns out my uncle and I wear the same size women's shoe. Dwayne helps me with the strap. I stand up in the heels. My knees buckle underneath me and I fall back onto the bed.

"Linda Evangelista is hanging her head in shame," Dwayne says. He pulls me to my feet. Dwayne takes me by the fingers and backs up as I walk toward him, like a parent teaching their child to walk. It's like I'm walking on stilts. I'm unsure of every step I take. I've never felt so awkward in all my life.

"I can't," I say.

"You can."

Dwayne lets go of my fingers, and I walk toward him holding my arms out like a tightrope walker. My feet *thunk thunk* against the hardwood floor as I start to find my balance. Baby steps become longer until I am actually walking in the heels. Not gracefully, but walking.

"Just a little more practice and you'll be strutting down the runways of Milan," Dwayne says.

"I don't know what that means."

"We are so watching *Fashion Television* together."

"Can I take these off now?" I say.

"Fine. But now it's time to do your makeup."

"Ah come on, Dwayne!"

"Tom, when will you ever do drag again?"

Never. Not if I can help it.

"Okay," I say. "But make it quick."

I show Dwayne where my uncle keeps his makeup. He sits me down on the toilet and starts covering my face in beige goop. I can feel my pores starting to clog up and my skin is getting warmer.

"Are you sure you know what you're doing?" I ask.

"I paint my mom's face all the time," he says.

"Have you ever gone out in public dressed like a woman?"

"No, but I would."

"What's stopping you?" I ask him.

"Fear of getting the shit kicked out of me. I'm practically a drag queen compared to most of the guys at my school. Close your eyes."

"I can't believe I'm saying this, but do you want to go out in drag tonight?" I ask.

"You'd do that?"

"As long I don't have to wear heels and we stay in the West End."

"Deal!"

"What the hell is going on in here?" Uncle Fred says from the bathroom door. "How many of those pot brownies did you guys eat?"

He stops yelling once he sees how we're dressed. His temper goes from furious to nearly falling over laughing.

Plaza of Nations

The line to get into the women's dance is the length of a football stadium. I feel like I'm looking at photos in a queer high school yearbook: bull dykes, femmes, rockers, jocks, activists. I search the line for Georgia, but I don't see her anywhere. I'm worried she won't come. That she's changed her mind. Again.

I came here with the team to celebrate our medal. Raven is already downstairs setting up for the dance. Cerise is already drunk, equal parts celebrating the bronze and trying to forget about Timbre. She's getting a little handsy with some of the other women on the team. Rhonda is looking out for her, like a den mother.

I can feel the air on my head. Nick the Barber shaved the back and the sides to a quarter inch. The top is parted to one side. I keep running my fingers through it, expecting to feel my shoulder-length hair. I'm worried what Mom will say when she sees it. Worried Georgia won't like it.

There's a "Woo-hoo!" from the front of the line as it lurches forward, down the escalator. We are greeted with a remix of "Tom's Diner" by Suzanne Vega. Raven is waving her hands over head. She's topless, and the women are loving it. Shirts and jerseys come off and are tucked into belt loops. The party has started.

I look around, trying not to seem desperate. I bob my head to the music. I do another sweep of the dance floor with my eyes and see Cerise coming toward me. Uh-oh. There's nothing worse than a drunk femme on the rebound. I can't tell if she's trying to look sexy or if she's trying to focus. I keep hoping Rhonda will swoop in and rescue me, but no such luck.

"Hey, Gina," Cerise says. She touches my nose with her finger. She's trying to be cute, but it comes off as sloppy.

"I like your haircut," Cerise says. "That new?"

"Just this afternoon."

Cerise puts her arms around me and starts to sway back and forth. Oh my God! Cerise, what are you doing? How do I let her down gently?

"I love a butch haircut on a woman," she says.

"Thanks. I've been wanting to do it for some time. I felt empowered by the bronze."

I'm trying to get out from Cerise's arms, but she's using me for support. I make eye contact with Raven in the DJ booth. "What the hell?" Her lips are saying. I shrug my shoulders, not knowing what to do.

"It was so sweet of you to cheer me on the way you did," Cerise says. "You didn't have to do that. I don't know if I could have if the shoe was on the other foot."

"I was just being a team player," I say. I'm starting to panic now. We just patched things up between us.

"You're more than just a teammate," she says. "You were a light in the storm and I want to show you how much I appreciate it."

Cerise pulls her jersey up over her chest, but it gets stuck on her medal and she can't get it over her head. She's not wearing a bra! Oh my god! Cerise's breasts are amazing. No wonder Timbre broke up with me.

"Gina?" Georgia says, her gold medal reflecting in the strobe lights.

"Georgia!"

"Cerise!" Rhonda says, emerging from the dance floor. She starts pulling Cerise's jersey back down over her boobs. Georgia is already leaving.

"Georgia, come back," I shout.

"I need a drink," Georgia says.

"You don't drink! You said so on the bus."

Georgia stops and looks me in the face. She looks hurt. Like she's about to cry. This whole week, I felt like she's been leading me on. Seeing her now, I can tell she was just as afraid of getting her heart stomped on as I was of mine.

"I know I was late getting here, but I didn't think you'd already be getting a lap dance," she says.

"She's my ex's ex. She's drunk. She's upset."

"Could have fooled me."

"It's the haircut! It has that effect on women."

"It does suit you better than that silly bandana," she says. "Is she really your ex's ex?"

"In this place? You couldn't throw a stone without hitting at least one."

"I know the type," she laughs. "Can we go someplace else? Someplace quiet. Bars aren't my scene."

I look around at all the women dancing and having fun. This is the Super Bowl of women's nightlife, and I'm being asked to give it up for I don't know what. Still, I say "Yes."

Outside, the hot air feels cool compared to inside the hall. Georgia takes my hand and we start walking toward the West End.

"What's with all the lions?" Georgia asks as we pass the Art Gallery.

"See those two peaks?" I say, pointing to the mountains

lit by the setting sun. "Those are the lions. They're named after a pair of Haida twins. They paved the way for peace between the Haida and the Squamish tribes."

"I'm impressed you knew that off the top of your head," she says.

"History was my favourite subject in school."

"Mine was home economics," Georgia says. "I'm a housewife at heart."

I stop and kiss her on the lips. She smells like Oil of Olay and Pantene. She strokes the back of my head. I feel like a cat curled up in its owner's lap.

We walk up Thurlow Street to Nelson Park. It's filled with gay and straight couples sitting on the benches, lying on the grass, staring at the stars. It's strange to see all these people at peace with each other. I put my arm around Georgia, and she nestles up against me.

Two messy drag queens are coming toward us singing "Everybody Dance Now!" One is wearing a denim mini skirt and a tube top. The other is wearing a muumuu and turban. Where do these guys get their images of women from?

"Gina?" the drag queen in the muumuu says.

"Dwayne?" I say. "Tom? Are you in drag?"

"I now go by Thumbelina," Tom says.

"Is there something in the water?" I say.

"Love," Tom says. "There's love in the water."

"We've had the most amazing day," Dwayne says.

"We ate pot brownies and listened to Sandra Bernhard. Then we went to The Dufferin and all these men started buying us drinks and then we ended up at The Gandy Dancer, and Tom came in second place in the drag contest."

"I was robbed!" Tom shouts. He lowers himself to the grass. "I need to lie down. The grass feels so cool."

"What you need is to go home and go to bed," I say. I turn to Georgia and ask her, "Do you mind if we take them back to his uncle's place? It's just around the corner."

"As long as they don't throw up on my shoes."

"We threw up on the way here," Dwayne assures us.

I help Tom to his feet and walk him back to the house on Bute Street. The house is unusually quiet. A man is sitting on the front steps of the porch.

"Tommy?" the man says into the dark.

Tom gets very sober very fast. "Dad?"

Friday, August 10, 2022

Bute Street

Dad follows me up the stairs to the spare room where Kouri was staying.

"Make sure you look like a man by the time I come back, Tommy," he says. Dad doesn't raise his voice when he's angry. He speaks above a whisper, like Clint Eastwood in *Dirty Harry*. I've never felt so humiliated in my life — and I've been hazed!

I rip the tube top as I struggle to get it off me. Sweat has glued the mini skirt to my thighs, and I topple over onto the floor as I pull it down over my knees. I can hear Dad arguing with Uncle Fred in the kitchen downstairs.

"You turned him into a fairy!" Dad says. "Who does that to his own nephew?"

"He was like that when he got here! I just gave him the space to be himself."

I drag my ass to the bathroom and turn on the shower to drown out their voices. I scrub at my face as hard as I can. Red, blue, and black inky water swirls down the drain. I massage shampoo into my hair and the smell of cigarette smoke latches onto the steam. I lean against the shower wall, then turn off the hot water to let the cold water sober me up. When I wipe the steam off the bathroom mirror, I see that my face looks like a finger painting. Dad will kill me if he sees me like this.

I go back to Kouri's old room and dive under the covers with my back to the door. I feel like such a faggot right now. I can hear those protestors from registration day screaming, "God hates fags!" I feel diseased, an outcast. This is exactly what I've been hiding from. This is what I thought I could run away from when I bought that plane ticket to Vancouver. I wish I could make these thoughts go away, but they won't. They just keep getting worse.

I try to cover my face with the pillow and pretend to be asleep when Dad comes back. He lies on top of the covers next to me. I can feel the tension of his body next to mine even though we aren't touching. He's still lying there like that when I wake up in the morning.

"I'm going to find a hotel room for us," he says. "I want you dressed and ready when I come back. We go home tomorrow. Clean up your face. You look like a clown."

I notice the pillow is stained with makeup. Dad leaves without saying goodbye. The sound of his footsteps ring like gongs as he goes back down the stairs. I wait until I hear the door close behind him before I leave the room.

Gaetan is standing in the hallway wearing nothing but a pair of Calvin Klein briefs.

"You okay?" he says to me.

I walk over and hug him tight. I hear myself sobbing. I try to force myself to stop, but I can't. This is the most normal I've felt since I came home last night.

"At least he didn't drag you to the nearest army recruiting centre," Gaetan says, patting my back.

"That's because they're not open yet," Uncle Fred says from his bedroom doorway.

"Hey, Uncle Fred," I say. "I'm really sorry this is happening. I never meant to turn your life upside down."

"Don't be sorry," he says. "This was a long time coming. It's what happens when the love that dare not speak its name screams, 'Look at me! I'm gay!'"

"It's like the elephant in the room took a shit on the floor," Gaetan says.

I start to laugh, but it hurts. I don't want to go back to the way things were. My whole life I've been taught how a man is supposed to act. How if you stray from that, it will send you down the path of ruin. But that's not what I saw this week. Everything I've ever known about the world has been undone. I don't want to go back to living a lie. But I have no choice. I was a fool for believing I ever did.

"You don't have to go," Uncle Fred says. "You can stay here with me. With us."

"I think it's best I go home," I say. "Things are pretty bad between you and my dad. Staying will only make it worse. If I go now at least you two have a chance of making up."

"Life is too short to waste time pleasing other people, Tommy," Gaetan says. "Tomorrow is not guaranteed."

"But he's my dad."

"That doesn't mean he knows what's best for you," Uncle Fred says.

"And you do?" I hear myself say.

"Well, maybe I'm not as wholesome as Uncle Henry from *The Wizard of Oz,* but I'm as fun and caring as Auntie Mame," Uncle Fred says. He goes back into his room, closing the door behind him with a thud.

Now I've pissed him off too. I sit down on the floor, trying to get my bearings. I feel like I have no family left to turn to.

"Put some Oil of Olay on your face," Gaetan says. "It will get the rest of the makeup off. I'll take care of your uncle."

I go back to the bathroom and find the Oil of Olay in the medicine cabinet. I rub the cream all over my face, thick as meringue, and let it seep into my pores. Its sharp scent clears my head a little. When I wash it off again, my face is clean except for a bit of faded eyeliner. I feel like my old self, but altered. It's my face in the mirror, but I'm looking at it with a different pair of eyes. I can go back to Mississauga and try to pretend I'm the same Tom I was a few weeks ago, but I wouldn't be fooling anybody, least of all myself.

I hear the phone ring. Uncle Fred answers it in his room.

"Tom!" he calls out. "It's Dwayne!"

I look back at my reflection in the mirror. Like Kouri said, best to rip off the band-aid.

"Tell him I'm still in bed."

Davie Street

Georgia is still asleep. I'm sitting on the balcony of her hotel room at the Mandarin Court Hotel with no shirt on, drinking a crappy cup of coffee from the machine down the hall. Davie Street is coming alive below me. Or coming home, in some cases. There are lines to get into Doll & Penny's and Hamburger Mary's. Stragglers are still coming home from the bars. There aren't as many people on the street as there were a couple of days ago. The city is emptying out. The Games are coming to a close.

"Morning, sunshine," Georgia says, pulling the sheets up to her shoulders. I don't know why she's covering herself; I've already seen her naked. "How long have you been up?"

"This long," I say, holding up my half-empty cup of coffee. "I couldn't sleep."

"I snore, I'm sorry."

"I'm used to snoring," I say. "I keep thinking about Tom and the look on his father's face last night. I'm worried I'm not going to see him again."

"We can check on him if you like," Georgia says.

"Do you mind?" I ask. "I already feel like I'm putting you out ... you helped drag him home and then you kicked your roommate out of the room."

"Don't worry about her," Georgia says. "She locked me out of the room a couple of nights this week. She has nothing on me. Let me grab a shower quick."

"Do you mind if I make a couple of local calls?" I ask her.

"Dial nine to get an outside line," Georgia says, wrapping the top sheet around her. She lets go of the sheet just as she's about to go into the bathroom allowing me one last glimpse of her naked body.

I call Dwayne first.

"Hey, buddy," I say when he picks up. "Have you talked to Tom this morning?"

"I tried, but no luck," Dwayne says.

"Georgia and I were going to head over to Fred's to see if he's still around," I say. "Want to come? We were going to get breakfast after, before the lines get too long."

"Can't. I'm volunteering down at Celebration Centre. There's a big choir concert today."

"I'll let you know if I hear anything," I tell him, and hang up the phone.

And now for the phone call I've been dreading. I take my time punching my home phone number into the dial pad.

"Where have you been?" Marcella says when she answers. "We were about to call the cops. We thought you were dead!"

"You guys think that whenever I leave The Drive."

"This isn't funny!" Marcella says. I can hear Mom's voice asking if it's me. The voice on the other end changes without warning.

"Gina! Come home now!"

"In a bit, I promise. I need to check on a friend."

"Your family are your friends. Come home now!" Mom slams the phone in my ear.

Georgia comes out of the bathroom wrapped in a towel. I'd be crying into the pillow if she weren't here right now. She gets dressed, and we take the elevator down to the lobby. The doors slide open, revealing Tom and his father. If Tom's dad recognizes me from last night he doesn't let it show. At first Tom looks happy to see me, and then it's like someone let the air of his smile, and he looks sad again. I step aside to let him onto the elevator. Our eyes meet as the doors close again.

"Wasn't that your friend?" Georgia says.

"I hope so."

Granville Street

There aren't as many gay couples holding hands on Granville Street. The ones that are blend in with the straight couples like this is already the new normal.

I'm worried about Tom. I hope Gina is able to find him and convince him not to go home to Ontario. His face reminded me of the time Mom introduced me to my good-for-nothing-father. He took one look at me, saw that I was a little gay boy, and couldn't drop me home fast enough. I'm worried Tom's father will enlist him in the army. Or enrol him in one of the camps that try to covert gay kids, like some of the teens I met at the LGBT Centre. I worry the moment he gets back to Ontario, he'll close the closet door on this part of his life. Instead of coming out, he'll get married, sneak around behind his wife's back, and get them both infected with HIV. Mom sees it all the time in the AIDS ward.

I make a pitstop at the Fluevog window. Madonna's Munster platforms have been replaced with a different shoe. The page has already turned on the Games.

"What did I say about you fogging up my window?" the manager says, poking his head through the door.

"I'm not standing anywhere near close enough to the windows to fog them up," I say.

"That's the best you've got? You sick or something?"

"Depressed," I say glumly.

He rolls his eyes like he's being forced to do something he doesn't want to do.

"Do you want to talk?" he says.

I look around like he's speaking to someone else.

"Why do you want to help me all of a sudden?" I ask him.

"Girl, as much as I hate to admit it, I was just like you when I was your age. I've stood in front of more than one window wishing I could afford what was on the other side."

"My friend is being dragged back to Ontario against his will," I blurt out.

"That cute guy I've seen you around town with?"

"He's more than just a pretty face," I say. I hate when people think of Tom as just an object.

"Don't get bent out of shape because of a guy. If these Games have taught me anything, it's that there are plenty of fish in the sea."

"This isn't about sex," I tell him. "But I wanted to have sex with him, believe me."

"Oh, I believe you. I cruised him like a hundred times this week. That boy doesn't get how hot he is, which makes him a hundred times sexier."

"Tell me about it," I say. "If he goes, I won't have any gay friends my age. Not like Tom at least. He's the first guy who didn't judge me by my looks or how I behave."

"How old are you?"

"Seventeen."

"You're probably sick of hearing this, but you're still young. You'll find what you're looking for. Trust me."

"Based on what?"

"Don't tell anyone this, but I'm getting transferred to San Francisco to manage the new Fluevog store on Haight Street."

"Get out!"

"I still can't believe it's happening."

"How did you manage that?"

"I'm good at what I do, girl! That's all you need to succeed in life. Just be good at what you do and everything else will fall into place."

"Congratulations, I guess," I say. "Who am I going to spar with after you're gone?"

"That would be Gilbert — or Geel-bear as he insists on being called. Total bitch. Not nearly as mean as me, but he'll keep your claws sharp."

"I don't even know your name," I say.

"Justin."

"Dwayne."

He offers me his hand to shake, but I hug him instead. He resists at first, and then hugs me back.

"I can put in a good word if you want a job," Justin says.

"I'm alright at A&B Sound," I say. "That store isn't going anywhere anytime soon."

I let go and start running down Granville toward the Plaza of Nations before I'm late for my volunteer shift. I don't know why Justin's transfer fills me with so much hope. Maybe I need a future to look forward to. Maybe I need to believe Vancouver won't go back to the way it was before the Games. Maybe I need to have more faith in Tom.

Davie Street

Our balcony at the Mandarin Court Hotel faces the mountains. The hotel pool is directly below us. The deck is crammed with sunbathers in tiny Speedos wearing sunglasses and gazing up at the sun. It looks like a carpet of flesh. One of the guys waves up to me. I wave back.

"Get away from there, Tommy," Dad says.

"But it's hot," I say.

"Let's get something to eat."

The restaurant lines are the shortest they've been all week. Dad notices the mustachio'ed mannequins on the canopy of Doll & Penny's Cafe.

"This town is depraved," he says.

Even the name "Hamburger Mary's" is offensive to him. We walk down the hill to the Grove Inn on Denman. There's hardly any line at all to get in. The waitress, a tiny blonde girl who reminds me of Chrissy from *Three's Company*, takes our order. Dad's shoulders are touching his ears he's so tense.

"Relax, Dad, this place isn't gay."

"Could have fooled me," he says. "Are you going to tell me why you were dressed like a cross-dressing hooker last night?"

"We were dressing up," I say.

"Dressing up is wearing a clown costume. Dressing up is tying a blanket around your neck and pretending you're Superman. You were acting like a fag."

It's not the first time Dad has used that word around me. It's not even the first time he's called me that when he was upset with me. But this is the first time he's said it about me and *meant* it.

"What's wrong with you?" he asks. "Why are you behaving this way?"

"Dad ..." The words are at the tip of my tongue. I just have to say them. Not just to Dad, but to myself. "I'm gay."

I feel like I'm floating off of my chair, dizzy from the sound of my own voice. Never in a hundred years did I think I'd be having this conversation with Dad. Not this soon. On his deathbed, maybe. Before I got on the plane to Vancouver, being gay was as bad as cancer. Now I feel like I've recovered from it.

"You're not gay. You've been corrupted," he says. "I blame Fred. I thought we could hide you from him, but he has a way of making everything about himself."

"Uncle Fred had nothing to do with it. I've been this way my entire life."

"You did a great job of hiding it."

"What choice did I have? How many times did you threaten to enlist me in the army if I was? It's like you suspected the whole time."

"You're telling me your uncle didn't lure you here with those birthday and Christmas cards?"

"No! It was Mom's *Village People*'s Greatest Hits tape. She left it in my car."

"What?" Dad says, slapping the table with his hand so hard the cutlery bounces.

Here we go again.

"I got in the car to go to work, and when I turned on the ignition, 'Go West' started playing. That was the seed that planted the idea in my brain to fly to Vancouver."

Dad looks around the diner like he can't believe what he's hearing.

"That was my tape!" Dad says. "I was looking for that tape! Are you telling me the Village People are gay?"

"Uh ... yeah, Dad ... they are."

"Not all of them, but most of them," says the older guy with leather suspenders seated at the table next to us. Dad glares at him. "Sorry," the man says, and goes back to his breakfast.

"So you're gay ... The Village People are gay," Dad

says, his voice louder than I'm comfortable with. "Is anyone else gay that I should know about?"

The people seated in our immediate vicinity raise their hands, as does the waitress who delivers our food.

West Hastings Street

"I really enjoyed that," I say to Georgia as we leave the Alison Bechdel reading. "*Dykes to Watch Out For* was my lifeline to the community while I was still figuring things out."

"Same here. Which character do you identify with most?"

"I go back and forth between Mo and Lois. I definitely have Lois's sex drive, but Mo's wardrobe and social skills."

"Interesting choices," Georgia says.

"What about you?"

"I see myself as a Toni. I like being around other lesbians, but I'm not into the bar scene. I definitely want a kid some day."

"You do?" I say, kind of surprised.

"Of course! I'm not letting my sexuality prevent me from becoming a mom."

"Why not adopt?" I say. "The planet is overpopulated as it is. I kind of feel it's our responsibility as queer people to even things out, you know?"

"I can't stand that word *queer*," Georgia says. "I'm not even thrilled with the word *lesbian*. I prefer *gay woman*."

I don't know what to say to that. I'm worried that if I challenge her on the word *queer* I might turn her off. I prefer an out-and-proud woman, but couples are allowed to have their differences, right?

"Want to check out Celebration Centre before it closes?"

"Might as well," she says. "I don't have anywhere to be now that the tournament is over."

We walk down to the glass-covered plaza. First we check out the Arts Fair. Turns out Georgia is really into scented candles and oils. I knew she was femme, but I wasn't expecting Blair from *Facts of Life*. Although I'm good with Blair from *Facts of Life*.

"So, when are you planning on showing your mother your haircut?" Georgia asks, holding a crystal to the light.

"I might wait 'til tomorrow until after the Games are over."

"Won't she worry?"

"She was born worried."

"That means she's doing her job," Georgia says, bumping into me on purpose.

"I really want to enjoy the rest of the Games," I say. "It's like every time I'm happy about something, she finds some way of making me feel bad about it."

"You can't hide from her forever," she says. "Who knows. Maybe she'll surprise you and like how you look."

"You don't know my mom," I say. "Mom and me

have been fighting this Cold War for months now. This haircut, it's like launching a nuclear bomb."

"You're right. I don't know your mom. But I do think you're being dramatic. It's just a haircut."

I'm tempted to remind Georgia that she's not out to her parents. And that she switched sports to avoid getting outed. I don't know how the Games haven't changed her. I'm not the same person I was before the Opening Ceremonies. I used to think Raven was too in-your-face about gay rights. But now that I've had a taste of what dignity feels like, I can see what it is all for.

"Dwayne said there's a big choir concert," I say to avoid telling Georgia how I really feel. "Let's to go check it out."

"Sure! It's been nearly an hour since I've heard 'Music of the Night' from *Phantom of the Opera*," Georgia says.

Plaza of Nations

With one day left of the Games, Mary Brookes is already planning how we are going to close up Celebration Centre. There are boxes of T-shirts and posters to be sold. Tomorrow they will go on sale at deeply discounted prices. Some of it belongs in the Museum of Vancouver. Something tells me it's going to be a long time before it gets there.

"Why don't you call it a day, Dwayne?" Mary says to me.

"I'm good. I don't have anything to do," I tell her.

"Baloney," she says. "Tomorrow is Closing Ceremonies. Enjoy the atmosphere while you can!"

I don't know what to do or where to go. I still have no idea where Tom is. Gina is off somewhere with Georgia. Once again, I'm on my own.

I walk toward the main stage. The men's and women's choirs have been performing most of the day. At this point I've heard most of the songs from *Phantom of the Opera* and *La Cage Aux Folles*. I'm not a huge fan of show tunes. I know that makes me a bad gay. I used to check out the *A Chorus Line* album from the library because of all the gay characters. I don't mind Gloria Gaynor's version of "I Am What I Am," but it's not something I would listen to outside of a gay club.

Listening to the choirs one right after another brought a lump to my throat more than once today. All those voices singing at once, chords rising to the sky, it was inspiring. I don't believe in God, but those songs were like prayers. Offerings to the universe to make AIDS go away and for those horrible right-wing politicians to stop using us as punching bags to get re-elected. Maybe some gay person locked up in a prison will hear our voices and find comfort in them — like Radio Free Europe during the war. Or not. Maybe the Gay Games are the most we can ever hope for. But I don't want to think like that. Not anymore.

I find a seat near the back of the performance area.

The Vancouver Men's Chorus is wrapping up "Anything Goes." The song ends, and the conductor welcomes the San Francisco Men's Chorus and the Seattle Men's chorus onto the stage. He turns to the audience and says, "We'd like to dedicate this last song to Dr. Tom Waddell and to our friends who did not live to celebrate with us this week."

The choir starts singing "Empty Chairs at Empty Tables" from *Les Misérables*. Mom took me to see the show at the Queen Elizabeth Theatre when it came to town. It was a really big deal for her, even though we were in the last row of the balcony. The song affected me when I heard it in the theatre, but hearing all these men questioning why they lived while their friends died sends hot tears down my cheeks. Around me, men and women are gulping back tears, exposing the sorrow that follows us around. It's not just AIDS. It's the bashings. It's the insults. It's the subtle forms of discrimination we put with up with for having a lisp or a swish. I don't want to go back to how it was before. I don't want to be a second-class citizen anymore. I don't want the Games to end.

"Hey, little buddy!" Gina says. "Why the long face?"

I get up from chair and hug her as tight as I can.

Beach Avenue

"What time is the flight home?" I ask Dad as we walk along the beach at English Bay. He keeps shielding his eyes from the shirtless men in spandex shorts and Speedos. I don't care what time we leave. We haven't talked since we left the Grove Inn a couple of hours ago. I can't stand the silence.

"We're taking the red-eye," he says. "It was the cheapest flight I could find. This little adventure of yours is costing me a fortune."

"That's a lot of time to kill," I say. "Want to watch some water polo at the Aquatic Centre?"

"Gay water polo?"

"The athletes are gay, but the water polo is the same," I say. He's probably picturing the Flamingo Race.

"What the hell," he says. "But if anyone hits on me, I'm hitting them back with my fist."

"That's the spirit," I tell him.

There are plenty of tickets available. Water polo's probably not as popular as swimming and diving because you only get to see the competitors from the shoulders up. It's a blessing in disguise. Dad doesn't feel as self-conscious as he did on the beach. We are able to find a place on the cement bleachers away from anyone else.

"Nice facility," Dad says. "I like the skylight."

"Too bad I'm going to leave before I had a chance to try it out."

"Don't try and guilt trip me," he says, watching the game. "Crap, those guys are pretty rough in the pool."

"Almost makes you want to show them a little respect," I say.

"Let's not get crazy."

"Uncle Fred competed in the Games."

"Get lost," he says.

"He did. Fifty- and hundred-metre breast stroke. I helped him train."

"Did he come in last?"

"Fifteenth and twenty-first," I tell him. "In the *world*."

Dad stops watching the game and looks at me to see if I'm lying. I put my right hand over my heart and hold my left hand in the air. Scout's honour. Dad nods his approval and goes back to watching the game.

"What are we doing here, Tommy?" Dad says, keeping his eyes on the pool. "Why did you go all this way and spend all this money to tell me what you are?"

"Because the moment I experience an emotion, you make me suppress it."

"I was teaching you to be a man."

"There's more to being a man than not crying. I can be gay and still be a man. Look at what's happening in this pool. Look at all these people living their lives. How much more proof do you need?"

"That's your uncle talking," Dad says. "You know he rents that house."

"So?"

"So? How is he going to retire?"

"I don't think Uncle Fred has retirement on his mind."

"Of course he doesn't. Why would he plan for the future?"

"Because he's HIV positive."

"He's what?"

"He has the virus that causes AIDS."

Dad slowly lowers his face into the palms of his hands. I've never seen him look so confused. I regret telling him. I didn't mean to. It slipped out. Or am I using Uncle Fred as a weapon? I'm not sure anymore.

"My brother has AIDS?"

"Just the virus."

"What's the difference?"

"I'm not entirely sure, but they're two different things. You can't tell him I told you though."

"So he's fine telling a seventeen-year-old he has AIDS, but he won't tell his own brother?"

"He doesn't know that I know."

"This keeps getting worse by the minute," he says. "You shared a bed with him!"

"That's not how you get it."

Dad gets up from his seat and starts walking toward the exit.

"Dad, wait!" I shout after him.

"I don't know anymore," he says, stopping in front of the sliding glass doors. "First you're gay, then the Village People are gay, and now my brother has AIDS. What's wrong with this world?"

"It's not the world, it's the people."

"I always wondered if he had it," Dad says. "He

seemed like the kind of guy who would. Never had a backbone. Always a weak kid."

"Uncle Fred is one of the strongest people I've ever met," I tell Dad. "He uses his legal degree to help people. He opens his home to people who need a place to stay. He's respected here. He's only a loser when he goes home."

Dad keeps walking out the glass door. "Do you know how to get to the hotel from here?"

"Follow me," I tell him.

I lead him to Bute Street. When we get to Pacific Boulevard, I look in the direction of Dwayne's house to see if I can catch a glimpse of him before I go home. No such luck. He's probably having the time of his life with Gina right now.

Back at the hotel, I flop onto the bed, willing the next few hours away. Dad grabs a beer from the mini-bar and sucks it back on the balcony. He's staring out across the horizon watching the boats on English Bay. I have no idea what he's thinking right now. He keeps telling me he's teaching me to act like a man, but he's acting like a baby. Screw this! I'm sick of trying to make this okay for him. I'm done trying to protect his feelings when he doesn't care the slightest about mine.

"I need a shower," Dad says abruptly.

I wait for the sound of the water, and then I sneak out of the room as quietly as I can. Out on the street, I cut across the parking lot of the Shoppers Drug Mart and take the alley to Bute Street. There's no point going back to my uncle's place, so I keep following the alley down the hill. I turn right and take Nicola until I get to Robson, to the only place no one I know in Vancouver will find me.

"I don't remember ordering room service," Kent says when I show up at his door.

Saturday, August 11, 1990
Closing Ceremonies

Third Avenue

I try sneaking into the house through my bedroom window, but it's locked. Mom is waiting for me in the living room when I enter through the front door. I can feel the heat of her anger from the couch. It's quiet. Everyone is still asleep.

"Gina! Where have you been?" she hisses. "And what have you done to your hair?"

"I was looking for a friend," I tell her.

This is true. After the concert at the Plaza of Nations, Dwayne, Georgia, and I took our chances and asked the front desk for the room number for "Schneider." To our amazement, he told us. I got the impression he had a lot of requests for room numbers this week. Tom's dad opened the door, expecting to see his son. It was tense, but he didn't slam the door in our faces. He told us that Tom had run away again, and he'd appreciate it if we let him know if we find him. I'm leaving out the part where I spent the night at Georgia's. Things are bad enough without Mom knowing that little detail.

"You and your friends!" Mom says. "I didn't have friends at your age. Aren't we good enough for you?"

"You don't even know me!" I say. "You keep trying to mold me into a five-year-old girl. Why can't you love me the way I am?"

"Because it makes me sick to see you like this," she says. She can't even look at me. Mom slumps her back into the couch like she's reached the end of a long journey. "I give up. I can't live like this. The fighting. The arguing. It's time to get your things and go."

"Can't I at least say bye to Dad and Marcella?"

"Another time. Leave."

I knew this was going to happen when I got my haircut. It's probably why I did it. To force Mom's hand. But not this suddenly. I feel like a stranger in my own home. Like a guest who overstayed her welcome by eighteen years. A freeloader. I go to my room and start filling my softball bag with clothes. Marcella comes into my room still wearing her nightgown.

"What's going on?" she asks.

"What does it look like?"

"Gina, stop. This is out of control," she says, trying to keep me from packing.

"Mom's right," I tell her. "We can't keep going on like this. We're going to end up hating each other more than we do."

"She doesn't hate you," Marcella says. "She just wants what's best for you."

"*This* is what's best for me," I say, running my hand through my hair. "I should have done it sooner. I didn't have the confidence until now."

I throw a few more things in my bag. I put my hand on my parents' bedroom door to say goodbye to Dad, but think better of it. If I don't leave now, I don't know if I will. Mom is still on the couch, her head in her hands. I walk out the door onto Third Avenue. Momentum carries me down the street and up Commercial Drive until I get to the SkyTrain station.

Raven isn't home when I ring the buzzer for her apartment. I walk back to Fred's house so I can leave a message on her answering machine. I'm relieved when the door opens. It's Tom's dad.

"Twice in twenty-four hours," he says. "I still haven't found him, if that's why you're here."

"I have no place else to go at the moment," I tell him. "Mind if I come in?"

To my surprise, he holds the door open for me.

Robson Street

I sit up in bed, my knees pulled close to my chest. I'm naked under the covers. A seaplane is taking off over the harbour. I've never felt so relaxed. So free. Kent is pacing the hotel room in his underwear.

"Have you seen my wallet?" he asks.

"No," I tell him. "What does it look like?"

He stops looking and says, "A wallet …" I can tell he wants to finish the sentence with "stupid" but stops himself.

"Did you try your pants?"

"First place I checked. You didn't take it, did you?"

"What makes you think I'd do something like that?"

"You're a runaway," he says nonchalantly. "Twice."

"That doesn't make me a thief," I say. "Is that it on the floor under the desk chair? Where your pants were hanging."

Kent bends over and picks his wallet up off the floor. "Must have blended in with the carpet. You're off the hook."

He's been antsy all morning. This whole week he couldn't get enough of me. Now it's like he can't wait to get rid of me. He was so happy when I showed up at his door last night. We started making out as soon I walked in the room. Any fears I had about having sex with a guy flew out the window as soon as our clothes hit the floor. It's strange how Dad kept trying to make a man out of me, but last night was the most masculine I've ever felt. I used every muscle in my body to get as close to Kent as I possibly could. When we finished, I was exhausted like after a game of water polo. I can't get enough of his body. But all he seems to care about is getting dressed.

"Want to go for breakfast?" I ask him. "Maybe a walk around Stanley Park?"

"I don't have time for breakfast. I have a plane to catch."

"You're not staying for the Closing Ceremonies?"

"If my plane is on time, I can make the beer bust at the Eagle wearing my medals."

"That's it? You're just going to leave me here?"

"I can't take you with me. I'd get arrested for transporting a minor across the border. Besides, we barely know each other."

"I thought you liked me."

"I do like you. Just the way you are right now."

"So Dwayne was right," I say. "You were only into me for sex."

"Tom, you're a good-looking boy and very smart, but I'm a lone wolf. I'm not looking for Mr. Right. I'm looking for Mr. Right Now. And when I'm old, I'll pay someone to be my boyfriend and take care of me. That's what makes America great."

There's a knock on the door.

"What now?" Kent says, getting the door.

Uncle Fred is waiting on the other side, a sour look on his face. I panic, pulling the sheets over my head, worried my father is with him.

"I can see you, Tommy," Uncle Fred says.

"How did you know where to find me?" I ask him.

"I've seen enough Doris Day and Rock Hudson movies to know how a romantic farce works," he says. "Your father was so worried about you, he asked me to help find you."

"As entertaining as this is," Kent says. "I'm still in my underwear with two strangers in my room and a plane to catch. If we could make this a road show, I'd really appreciate it."

"That's it?" Uncle Fred says to Kent. "That's all he gets? You were the first person he had sex with."

"Seems like it was pretty memorable, if you ask me," Kent says.

I don't know what hurts more: going back to Mississauga or knowing I let Kent lead me on even though everyone warned me what he was doing.

"Can you guys turn around while I get dressed at least?" I ask.

I put on my clothes feeling like a fool. Uncle Fred puts his arm around my shoulder as he leads me out the door. I stop. Kent looks pissed off. This is how he probably looked when he told Dwayne he was a nobody.

"Did you ever vote for Reagan?" I ask Kent.

"Twice," he says.

That's all I need to know.

Jervis Street

Uncle Fred takes me to a restaurant that looks like a small house built into the side of the hill. Our waiter is this mean French-Canadian guy with a bushy moustache who reminds me of Gaetan's evil twin. Coffee spills over the lip of the mug as he pours it.

"If you want more, it's over there," he says, pointing at the machine in the corner, and walks away.

"So much for service with a smile," I say.

"He owns the place, and he makes the best pancakes in town," Uncle Fred says. "I wish I could have been as rude as he was when I was waiting tables in university."

"If you're trying to butter me up with pancakes so I'll talk to Dad, it's not going work. I'm not going home."

"Then you need to tell him to his face."

"You didn't," I remind him. "You ran away as far you could and you turned out okay."

"Did I?" he says. "Look at where we are. I had to keep your Dad from calling the cops. Could you imagine if they had shown up at the hotel instead of me?"

My spoon makes a clanking sound as I stir my coffee and picture it. Kent could have been arrested if they found out we had sex. I would have hated for that to have happened even after the way he treated me at the hotel.

"Stop that!" our waiter shouts from the other side of the restaurant.

"I'd listen to him," Uncle Fred says.

"He's so mean!" I whisper.

"I know that you know that I'm positive," Uncle Fred says.

"How?"

"I had my suspicions when you were helping me with the race," he says. "But I knew for sure when your father told me this morning after he showed up at my door unannounced."

"Does Gaetan know you know he told me?"

"That guy!" Uncle Fred says, slapping the table. "This is exactly why he used to always get arrested when he was hustling. He never knew when to keep his mouth closed!"

"I don't want you to die," I say.

"Oh shut up!" he says. "I'll be here with Cher and the cockroaches after you're all dead."

"I don't know what that means."

"One day you will, and you will be a better person for it. But for now, we're going to eat some pancakes, and then you're going to tell your dad what you want to do. No more running away."

The waiter drops two heavy plates of pancakes an inch from the table's edge. The coffee sloshes around in our mugs and our cutlery rattles.

"How does he stay in business?" I ask.

"Taste the pancakes," he says.

The first bite melts in my mouth.

"These are the best pancakes I've had in my life."

"Eat up," Uncle Fred says. "You're going to need your strength when you talk to your father. And Nurse Ratchet over there will force you to make a donation to the Persons with AIDS Foundation."

I look over at our waiter who's adding up bills.

"What the hell do you want?" he barks.

"Nothing."

"Eat your breakfast," he says. And then he smiles.

Bute Street

I'm sitting on the couch across from Tom's dad on the recliner. It's hot. The whir of the two square fans fills the silence between us. I don't know how old Tom's Dad is, but he looks good for someone with a seventeen-year-old kid. It's like looking into the future to see what Tom will look like at his age. I wonder if we'll still be friends when that happens. I hope so.

"So … how do you like Vancouver so far?" I ask, breaking the silence.

Tom's dad looks at me like I've got to be kidding. I smile politely.

"What did you say your name was again?"

"Gina."

"Well, Gina, Vancouver is pretty," he says, almost robotically. "I'll give Vancouver that. I didn't know my brother lived so close to the beach."

"Nothing better than Vancouver in the summer."

"You've never been to Muskoka," he says. He loosens up as if realizing I'm not the enemy he thought I was. "So how do you know my son?"

"I met him here on my birthday. My friend Raven is Fred's best friend. Me, Tom, and Dwayne have been hanging out ever since."

"I'm guessing you're gay too."

"Queer as a three-dollar-bill. I'm guess you're hoping that something happened between me and Tom?"

He laughs. "A little."

"If it makes you feel better, I'd totally date Tom if I wasn't gay."

"I guess that's something."

Tom's dad leans forward in the recliner and rubs his temples. He looks like Mom did when I was leaving the house. I'm a little worried for Tom now. And I feel kind of sorry for his dad. It reminds me of how things started to go sideways between Mom and me.

"How are your parents with you being gay?" he asks.

"I left home this morning."

"I need a drink," he says.

"It's only ten in the morning," I remind.

"Who's the adult here?" he snaps.

"You tell me," I snap back. Last thing I need is him unloading his baggage on me.

"Did you play any sports in these so-called Gay Games?" he says, calmer now.

"Fast pitch."

"Tom played softball back home."

"He umpired a few games in the tournament. He called a strike on me that I'm still convinced was a ball."

"My Tommy knows a strike when he sees one," he says, proud of his son again. "How'd you do in the tournament?"

"Bronze."

"Not bad!"

"Not gold."

"A woman after my own heart," he says. He gets up from the recliner and looks out the front window like he's expecting Tom to show up at any minute. "What are we even talking about? It's like last week the world was one thing and now it's something else completely."

"Try being gay," I tell him. "Tomorrow the world goes back to the way it was for us. I finally got to experience what it's like to be the majority. Everything we do is prefaced with the word *gay*. Gay bar, gay restaurant, gay games. All we're doing is living our lives."

Tom's dad seems to consider this.

"Do you ever plan on talking to your parents again?"

I was in such a hurry to get out of the house, I never

thought about what I was going to do this afternoon, much less tomorrow.

"Eventually, I guess. Not for a couple of weeks."

"To punish them, eh?"

"Too cool off."

"I'm not leaving here without my son," he says.

There's a knock on the door. I gesture to Tom's dad that I'll get it. Dwayne is standing on the other side.

"Why aren't you at home getting ready for the closing ceremonies?" he says.

"Long story," I whisper. "Tom's dad is here."

"Where's Tom?" he whispers back. I shrug.

"I can hear you!" Tom's dad shouts.

"Come on in," I say to Dwayne. He looks nervous as he walks into the house.

"Hey there," Dwayne says, polite as can be. He offers his hand for Tom's dad to shake. "We met last night, remember?"

Tom's dad looks at Dwayne like he's his worst nightmare.

"Weren't you the kid in the dress with my son?" he asks him.

"That old thing?" Dwayne says. "It was on the floor when I woke up."

The screen door opens again.

"Found him!" Fred shouts. He looks surprised when he sees the three of us in the front room. "The gang's all here."

Tom has a hangdog expression on his face until he notices me and Dwayne.

"What are you guys doing here?" he asks.

"Selling Avon," Dwayne says.

"Come on, Tom," his dad says. "It's time we got going."

"Can I at least say goodbye to my friends?" he asks.

"Make it quick," his dad says.

"Give them some space," Fred says to Tom's dad. We wait until the two of them have gone to the kitchen.

"I guess this is it," I say.

"I can't believe I'm not going to the Closing Ceremonies. I feel ripped off," Tom says.

"I'm going to miss you," Dwayne tells him.

"Same," I say.

"I wish it wasn't so expensive to call," Tom says.

"We can write," Dwayne says.

"I'm terrible at writing letters," Tom says.

"So this is the end?" I ask.

"Maybe," Tom says. "For now, at least. Something tells me Dad is going to be keeping a very close eye on me when I get home."

"I just spent the last thirty minutes with him," I say. "He's not a bad guy. There's hope for him."

"He's not a bad guy," Tom says. "He's just set in his ways."

The three of us embrace in a group hug. I knew that Tom would go home at some point; I just never imagined it would be like this.

"Ready, Tommy?" his dad says, interrupting the hug.

"I guess so," he says.

Me, Dwayne, and Fred follow them out to the front porch. Tom looks back at us as they go through the gate one last time. We wait a minute, half expecting him to come running back, but he doesn't. The Closing Ceremonies are still a few hours away, but the Games already feel like they're over.

Comox Street

"This is where I get off," Gina says, standing in front of Raven's apartment building at the corner of Bute and Comox. She called ahead to make sure Raven was home before coming over.

"You can get ready for Closing Ceremonies at my place if you like," I tell her. "Mom won't mind."

"You just want to make me over, don't you, Dwayne?" she says skeptically.

"A little eye shadow never hurt anyone," I tell her. "And I wouldn't mind the company."

"You'll be okay, little buddy," she says. "You heard Fred. Tomorrow we'll all go down to Second Beach Pool and pretend like the Games never ended."

Easy for Gina to say. She has Georgia to spend the last night of the Games with. I don't have anybody. I was jealous of her last night after we gave up trying to find Tom. Gina gave me her tickets to GAYLA, the celebration of women's culture concert at the Orpheum, so she could spend the night with Georgia. I invited Justice to make up for how I treated him this week. We had a good time, but I still feel sad. Now that I know how good things can be, I don't want them to go back to the way they were.

I walk to Stanley Park to watch the end of the marathon. This and tennis are the last events of the Games. There are more spectators than I expected, cheering the runners as they pass by. There are competitors from all walks of life. The die-hards in high-cut running shorts and tank tops like in the Olympics, and big-hipped women in baggy shorts, Ts, and caps, like you'd see jogging down the street. And then there are people in wheelchairs doing their thing like everyone else. It's beautiful.

I find a spot near the finish line and clap and cheer for the runners, even though I don't know anyone in the race. The runners have anguished faces as they cross the finish. They fall into the arms of the friends and loved ones who have supported them in getting here. I think of the sacrifices they made, the hours of hard work they put in so they would have the strength to finish. It fills me with hope and reminds me how far we've come as a community in four years. It's a reminder that freedom is not a race, it's a marathon.

"Hey, Dwayne!"

It's Warren from school. I haven't seen him since he

stopped by the information booth at Celebration Centre.

"Hey!" I say.

"I was hoping I'd run into you before the Closing Ceremonies," he says. "I wanted to let you know how impressed I was by the Games. I'm amazed at what you guys were able to accomplish this week."

"I was just a volunteer," I say bashfully.

"It doesn't matter," he says. "It took a few days, but I finally got what the Games were about. I got to experience how it feels to be a minority. There were times when I really hated it, but for the most part, people were pretty welcoming and accepting. I get why this was so important to you guys. I mean, if gay people can't even get together to play sports, then what can they do, right?"

"Right," I say. "I'd say our work here is done, but it feels like it's only just beginning."

"Want to hang out for a bit?" Warren asks.

"I need to go home and get changed," I tell him. "I'm volunteering at the Closing Ceremonies."

"I'll walk back to Denman with you," he says.

It's the first time he's asked to hang out without my hoping he would kiss me. It's sad in a way, but it frees me to get to know Warren as something other than a crush. I only wish Tom stayed in Vancouver long enough to have had the same experience with him.

Davie Street

Dad and I are lying on our beds, watching the six o'clock news. I've been trying to find the guts to tell him I don't want to go home, but I'm afraid that if I do, he'll never speak to me again. Twice now I've gone to the bathroom to rehearse what I want to say in the mirror. Both times he knocked on the door to ask, "What are you doing in there?"

I'm ready to throw in the towel. Be a good son and keep the peace. But the thought of getting on that plane and pretending that Vancouver and the Gay Games never happened depresses me.

I go out onto the balcony for some air. It's my last sunset in Vancouver. The sky is streaked with pinks and purples. I can see people on the beach waiting for the sun to dip below the mountain peaks. Tomorrow I'll be back in muggy Mississauga, where I'll have to drive a car to go to the beach. What I'll miss most about Vancouver is the freedom to walk everywhere.

Freedom. I hear that word so often in songs, movies, by generals, and politicians, but I didn't understand what it meant until now. I think of Uncle Fred, saving his energy for the home stretch and pulling ahead of some of the swimmers. He may not have finished first in his division, but he finished strong, like he intended to do. Now it's my turn to take my own advice. My turn to follow in his footsteps.

"Dad," I say as I go back into the room. "There's something I need to say …"

The news cuts to an on-the-scene reporter at BC Place Stadium. He's interviewing people as they arrive for the Closing Ceremonies. I notice that some spectators are hiding their faces from the camera so they won't be recognized. The people who are willing to speak to the reporter tell him how proud they are of the community and the city for putting on a successful Games. Then the reporter holds his microphone to Dwayne's face. He's wearing his blue volunteer shirt and waving to the camera.

"Isn't that your friend with the Zorro hat?" Dad asks from his place on the bed.

"That's Dwayne," I say.

"What has Celebration '90 meant to you?" the reporter asks Dwayne.

"Expo '86 may have put Vancouver on the map," Dwayne says, "but the Gay Games brought Vancouver into the twentieth century. And if you're watching this, Tommy, I love you and I'm going to miss you! This has been the best summer of my life!"

The reporter pulls the microphone away from Dwayne's face as fast as he can. I guess hearing a guy telling another guy he loves him is still too much for the evening news. Dad clicks the TV off.

"I can't do it," he says. "I can't go back to Mississauga with you. Not like this."

"Are you letting me stay? Or are you kicking me out of the house?"

"I don't have an answer for that yet."

"Do you hate me?"

"No," he says. "But after watching your friend on TV just now, I'm afraid if I take you home right now that I will."

I sit down on the bed. This is exactly what I didn't want to happen. To my surprise, Dad puts his hand on my shoulder.

"Your friend Gina said something to me today that stuck with me," Dad says. "She said no matter what you guys do, straight people always put the word 'gay' in front of it. I need time to stop thinking about you as my *gay* son and as just my son."

"What if you never get there?" I ask him.

"We'll get there," he says. "We'll keep cheering for the home team until we do."

Dad hugs me, squeezing me tighter than he ever has before. I wish he wasn't hugging me goodbye.

"You should go be with your friends," Dad says. "I'll drop your things off at your uncle's before I leave."

I walk and then run down the hall to the elevator. The tears that roll down my face are hot and sting. The elevator can't come fast enough. The hotel lobby looks like the last day of summer camp. People are standing next to their luggage, saying their goodbyes.

Outside, the sidewalk is clogged with people cruising and barhopping, soaking up what is left of the Games. I try to get on a bus, but it's packed. So I start to jog, and then run, toward the stadium. I'm completely out of breath by the time I get to BC Place Stadium. I see Dwayne standing near one of the gates talking to the volunteer coordinator.

"Dwayne! Dwayne!" I wheeze, trying to get my second wind. He's stunned to see me.

"What are you doing here?"

"I'll tell you later. Where's Gina?"

"Inside the tunnel waiting to enter the stadium."

"Think we can find her?"

"We can try!" He turns to Heather, the volunteer coordinator, and asks, "Do you mind if we enter with the athletes?"

"Be my guest," she says.

Dwayne takes my hand and we start running into the stadium entrance. We go down a few winding halls and end up in a giant tunnel beneath the field. A volunteer lets us on to an elevator that feels as big as my house. The elevator comes to a stop, and we run out. Ahead of us we can see the end of the procession of athletes entering the stadium. We reach them just as they enter the stadium to cheers from the stands. I know the cheers are for the athletes, but I can't help but feel they're cheering for me and Dwayne as well.

BC Place Stadium

I'm holding Georgia's hand as we enter the stadium. I notice she isn't squeezing it as tight as before. There's as much joy among the athletes as there was for the Opening Ceremonies, but it's tinged with sadness. I assume Georgia is coming down from the excitement of the last week. It's no secret Gay Games IV will be held in New York City to honour the twenty-fifth anniversary of the Stonewall Riots, four years from now. It's something to look forward to, but it feels like an eternity.

All around us, athletes are trading buttons and pins from their home cities, exchanging addresses, making plans to see each other again. But I only have eyes for Georgia.

"Once I'm settled and have my own place, I'll start saving my money to come visit you in Boston," I tell Georgia. "Maybe we can go to Cheers."

"You know that's not where they film the show, right?" she says.

"I know, but I'd still like to see it."

"Let me get home first before we start making plans," she says.

"Oh, for sure," I say. "But I can call you, right?"

"Won't that be expensive?" Georgia laughs, pulling her hand out of mine and putting it on my shoulder. Something's different. Something's changed. I can sense it. I felt it before on our way to the stadium, but I thought I was imagining it. I feel like I've been here before. With Timbre.

"What time is your flight out tomorrow?" I ask her.

"Eight in the morning," she says.

"Mind if I come with you to the airport to see you off?"

"I'm not sure that's a good idea," she says.

"Can we at least spend tonight together?"

"I don't think that's a good idea either."

"What's going on? Why are you acting so different?"

"Gina … I haven't been entirely honest with you …" Georgia says. "My name's not Georgia. It's Stephanie. And I don't play basketball for the national team, I play soccer."

"Why're you telling me this now?"

"Because if I do make it to the Olympics, I don't want you to see me on TV knowing that I lied to you," she says. "You're special, no matter what your mom thinks or says."

"I don't feel special. In fact, right now I feel the exact opposite."

"But you are," she says, starting to cry. "Even when you were wearing that stupid bandana to hide your hair. You deserve to be with someone brave enough to live out loud. That's not me. I don't know if it ever will be."

"I need to go," I say.

"Gina! No! Let's just enjoy these last few hours."

I look into Georgia's, or Stephanie's, face. I don't even know who I'm looking at anymore. I kiss her and run back toward the entrance to the stadium.

"Gina!"

At first I think it's Stephanie calling my name.

"GINA!"

That's a guy's voice. That's Tom's voice.

I see Tom and Dwayne running toward me from the tunnel. I jump into Tom's arms, and he swings me around. He puts me down and Dwayne jumps on top of me. My heart is still broken, but I can already feel it starting to mend. The three of us jump up and down, like we just scored the winning goal in a game, the crowd cheering. And then we put our arms around each other in a huddle, foreheads touching, ready to take on the world.

Sunday, August 12, 1990

Bute Street

The world looks the same as it did yesterday, but it's different. Uncle Fred is rushing around making sure he has everything for our picnic at Second Beach Pool. Gina, Raven, Gaetan and I are in the living room cooling off in front of the fans and listening to Dusty Springfield sing "I Think It's Gonna Rain Today."

"We're just going swimming, not to the Last Supper," Gaetan shouts at my uncle.

"I'm making sure the kids have plenty to eat," he shouts from the kitchen.

"They're not kids," Raven says. "They're teenagers. And they already know more than we did at their age."

"I'm always down for a snack," I say.

"That's the ticket, Tommy," Gina says. "Delay your uncle even more."

I hear the screen door open and swing close again. Dwayne walks into the living room with his mother.

"Sorry we're late," Dwayne says. "I invited Justice. He called this morning and said he needed to give me something. He should be here any minute."

"At the rate Fred is going, this could be a sunset swim," Raven says.

The doorbell rings.

"Come in!" the five of us shout. It's Justice. I almost don't recognize him in his Hawaiian shirt and trunks. He's holding a shoebox.

"Hey, everybody," he says, waving meekly. He hands the shoebox to Dwayne. "Some guy dropped this off at the store last night."

"What guy?"

"Bald guy with muscles," Dwayne tells him. "Said his name was Justin from Fluevog."

"No!" Dwayne says, throwing open the lid of the shoebox. He pulls out a pair of clunky women's shoes that look they belong in another century. "Oh my God! This is the best day of my life!"

"I hope you're not planning on wearing those to the pool," I say as Dwayne tries them on.

"They fit!" Dwayne says. "How did he know my size?"

"Honey, if there's one thing a gay guy in a shoe store

can tell by looking at you, it's the size of your foot," Gaetan says.

"All set?" Uncle Fred says. "I hope we can still find a good spot at the pool away from those horrible children."

Everyone gets their things together, and we trundle out of the house in a blob.

"I feel like the Von Trapp family singers," Dwayne says.

"But gayer," Gina says.

We wait for the light at the corner of Jervis and Davie. The people in the Celebration '90 poster smile back at us, inviting us to come celebrate with them.

"And to think, they didn't want to use the word *gay* in that poster," Uncle Fred says.

"The city had no idea how much money they were going to make off of us," Raven says with a hint of bitterness.

"All that fuss over a word," Gina says.

"Never again," Dwayne says. "We are here to stay."

Historical Note

When creating the timeline of events for this novel, I used the listings in both *Angles*, Vancouver's queer newspaper at the time, and the official program of the 1990 Gay Games. With minor exceptions, the athletic and cultural events occurred on the dates and times recorded in the novel. While I would have preferred my characters to attend more events, there were too many for one book.

The depictions of Bill Monroe, Richard Dopson, Betty Baxter, Fraser Biggs, Daniel Collins, Heather Williams, and Mary Brookes are based on the interviews I conducted while researching the book. Any dialogue attributed to them is a work of fiction inspired by those conversations. As well as Richard Dopson and Betty Baxter, the Board of Directors for the Metropolitan Vancouver Athletics & Arts Association included Bill Amundsen, Will Bennest, Corren Douglas, Barry McDell, and Ruth Lea Talk. The executive director of Gay Games III was Mark Mees. Although these individuals do not appear in the novel, their contributions to the Games were essential to their success.

Josephine's Cafe was a real coffee shop. However, the shop was not in business during the 1990 Gay Games.

Lastly, this is a novel about a diverse community demanding a seat at the table. They did so by working through their differences to host one of the world's largest sporting events in 1990 without financial support from federal and provincial governments, without advertising, and without the benefit of the Internet. Any discussion of conflicts that surfaced during the organizing and hosting of Gay Games III/Celebration '90 and that are addressed in this novel are intended to demonstrate the value of cooperation for the benefit of the common good.

And yes, there really was a double rainbow for the Opening Ceremonies.

-TC

Resources

Books:

Gay Olympian: The Life and Death of Dr. Tom Waddell
By Tom Waddell and Dick Schapp
Alfred A. Knopf, 1996.

The Spirit Captured: The Official Photojournal of Celebration '90 — Gay Games III & Cultural Festival
Contributors Forzley, Richard; Hughes, Douglas; Kent Kallberg Studios
For Eyes Press, c1990.

Online Resources:
Celebration '90: Gay Games III
VIVO Archive
http://archive.vivomediaarts.com/gay-games-iii/

Celebration '90: Gay Games III & Cultural Festival
Digital Museums Canada, Community Stories Collection
https://www.communitystories.ca/v2/celebration-1990-canadas-gay-games_gay-games-du-canada/

We Are Here to Stay!!!
City of Vancouver Archives
Copyright: Scintilla Productions;1990
https://searcharchives.vancouver.ca/we-are-here-to-stay

Documentaries:
Light in the Water
2018
Director: Lis Bartlett

Athletic organizations:
Federation of Gay Games
https://gaygames.org

West End Softball Association (WESA)
http://www.wesa.net/

English Bay Swim Club
https://www.englishbay.org

Acknowledgements

The author would like to thank the team at Lorimer, particularly my editor, Allister Thompson, for his confidence in these characters and for keeping this book moving forward. I'd also like to thank Carrie Gleason for putting forward the idea of writing a novel about queer history in Canada from a youth's perspective.

A big thank-you to my brother from another mother, Billeh Nickerson, who will always tell me what I don't want to hear and remind me of my worth in equal measures ("Fight the Power!"). Shout out to my peeps Mette Back and Dean Mirau ("Hello-tus!"). To Mark Kokocki who does more to promote my books than I do. Thank you for your copy of *The Spirit Captured*. To Ken Boesem: I can't thank you enough for your copy of the official program for the 1990 Gay Games. And to Tania Alekson for your research tips. Thanks to Justin Quonson and Art Goulet of WESA for connecting me with softball players who participated in the Games and for the photos of the softball tournament.

I would like to thank the following individuals for taking the time to do interviews about the Gay Games: Richard Dopson, Betty Baxter, Mary Brookes, Fraser Biggs, Daniel Collins, Tom Quigley, Colin McTavish, and Bill Bader. I would also like to thank the members of the Vancouver Gay History Facebook page for posting their photos, videos, and memories. Thank you for keeping our stories alive.

And to my niece, Jackie Dasilva: Remember to think of the beautiful future ahead.